Welcome to the Secret World of Alex Mack!

One of my best friends is in big trouble, but she doesn't even know it! The guys from the plant think she's me. I mean, not me, but the person they're looking for is me, not her, but they don't know that. Are you confused? Let me explain:

I'm Alex Mack. I was just another average kid until my first day of junior high.

One minute I'm walking home from school—the next there's a *crash!* A truck from the Paradise Valley Chemical plant overturns in front of me, and I'm drenched in some weird chemical.

And since then—well, nothing's been the same. I can move objects with my mind, shoot electrical charges through my fingertips, and morph into a liquid shape . . . which is handy when I get in a tight spot!

My best friend, Ray, thinks it's cool. And my sister Annie thinks I'm a science project.

They're the only two people who know about my new powers. I can't let anyone else find out—not even my parents—because I know the chemical plant wants to find me and turn me into some experiment.

But you know something? I guess I'm not so average anymore!

The Secret World of Alex Mack™

Alex, You're Glowing!
Bet You Can't!
Bad News Babysitting!
Witch Hunt!
Mistaken Identity!

Available from MINSTREL Books

Mistaken Identity!

Diana G. Gallagher

A MINSTREL® BOOK

Published by POCKET BOOKS
New York   London   Toronto   Sydney   Tokyo   Singapore

A MINSTREL PAPERBACK *Original*

 A Minstrel Book published by
POCKET BOOKS, a division of Simon & Schuster Inc.
1230 Avenue of the Americas, New York, NY 10020

Copyright © 1996 by Viacom International Inc., and RHI Entertainment, Inc. All rights reserved. Based on the Nickelodeon series entitled "The Secret World of Alex Mack."

ISBN: 0-671-55778-5

First Minstrel Books printing February 1996

10 9 8 7 6 5 4 3 2 1

Cover photo by Blake Little

Printed in the U.S.A.

For Tim Hruszkewycz,
in great appreciation
for his interest and advice

CHAPTER 1

"What do you say, Alex?"

"Huh?" Alex Mack stopped walking and looked up at the sound of her name. She had been staring at the sidewalk, so totally lost in thought that she didn't have a clue what her three friends were talking about. She was certain she had failed a surprise quiz in her seventh-period math class, and that the B average she had struggled so hard to maintain had suddenly turned into a C.

"Do you want to go with us?" Robyn Russo asked again.

Alex blinked. "Go where?" she asked, noting the worried frown on the slim girl's pale, freckled face.

Nicole Wilson and Raymond Alvarado exchanged a quick glance before they too gave her a curious stare.

"Earth to Alex," Nicole said, leaning forward to peer at Alex through intense brown eyes. "We're going to the mall today and you are cordially invited, unless you plan to be in another galaxy."

"The mall . . ." Alex repeated absently.

"Yeah. You know, the mall," Raymond said brightly. "It's a bunch of stores all clumped together in—"

"I know what a mall is, Ray!" Alex snapped.

Raymond's smile faded. "Cool your jets, Alex. I was just kidding."

"Sorry," Alex said with genuine regret. She knew it wasn't right to jump all over her best friend just because she was in a bad mood. "I am sorry, Ray. Really."

"That's okay," he said. "I noticed you haven't exactly been your usual cheerful self today."

2

"Too true," Nicole said, brushing a wisp of black hair off her dark face. "So what's the problem, Alex?"

"Nothing." Switching her backpack to her other shoulder, Alex started off down the sidewalk again.

"Well, something must be wrong," Raymond insisted as he and the two girls caught up.

"I really don't want to talk about it, okay?" Alex quickened her pace. Discussing her problems and shortcomings was not going to make them go away, or make her feel better.

Her parents had decided to give Alex total control over her daily life, hoping that would make her more organized and responsible. Her older sister, Annie, had approved wholeheartedly. Alex herself had to admit it was a great idea. After all, she was fourteen and in the eighth grade. It was about time her family started treating her like an adult.

But nothing had gone right since she had gotten up that morning.

When Alex slept through her alarm, Annie didn't wake her like she usually did. Then Alex discovered she'd forgotten to do her laundry the night before. Wearing wrinkled, dirty jeans and a striped T-shirt, she had barely made it to school on time, and in her panicked haste to get out of the house, she had left an overdue library book lying on the kitchen counter. The librarian had revoked her checkout privileges for a week, and the day had gone downhill from there.

Alex sighed again. It was a beautiful afternoon for mid-February. The sun shone brightly in a cloudless sky, taking some of the chill out of the light breeze. Alex, however, was too troubled to enjoy the unusually pleasant winter weather.

"Maybe you're coming down with that bug that's going around school, Alex," Robyn suggested.

"It's probably another new, exotic virus that will completely baffle the medical community," Nicole said, "if we don't all croak first, that is. Every time people go into an unexplored part of the globe and start disturbing the ecological balance, dormant and previously unknown microorganisms are awakened and released on the world." Nicole got worked up over some new issue every other week, and this time it was ecology.

"Maybe." Robyn scowled thoughtfully. "Or maybe Paradise Valley Chemical is pumping something toxic into the air. Who knows what they're cooking up in there."

"Yeah, who knows." Raymond shot Alex a sidelong glance.

Actually, Alex knew a whole lot about Paradise Valley Chemical, but she didn't want to talk about that, either. And even if she wanted to, she *couldn't* talk about it. Only Raymond and Annie knew that she had acquired some really strange abilities after being doused with the secret compound the plant had developed.

Alex glanced at Robyn and Nicole. They were both staring at her like she might suddenly sprout wings and fly. She couldn't, of course, but she could do a lot of other things that were just as fantastic. She wondered, not for the first time, how Robyn and Nicole would feel about having a best friend who could move things just by thinking about it and send small bolts of electricity shooting from her fingers. The fact that

Alex could change into a glob of silvery ooze at will didn't bother Raymond, but then, he thought all her powers were cool.

Robyn, however, viewed everything as a worst-case scenario. If she knew the truth about Alex, she'd probably envision all kinds of disastrous consequences Annie hadn't even considered. And Annie was a science whiz kid. Nicole, champion of truth and justice, would insist that Alex expose the plant's dangerous activities—something Alex absolutely could not do.

"Are you feeling nauseous or feverish or anything?" Robyn asked.

"I'm not sick, I swear." Alex forced a smile.

"You sure?" Raymond asked.

"Yes, I'm sure. It's just been a majorly rotten day."

"Well, that's a relief." Robyn grinned. "It would be a shame if you had to miss the Valentine's dance tomorrow night."

"I haven't decided whether to go or not anyway," Alex said.

"Because Scott is going with Kelly?" Robyn asked.

Alex just sighed and kept walking. A year older than her, Scott was incredibly nice and too handsome for words. Alex liked him—a lot. But even though he didn't have a steady girlfriend now that Jessica had moved out of town, he *was* taking Kelly to the dance.

"Scott's not the only boy in the world, Alex," Robyn said. "I happen to know that Michael Murphy has a major crush on you. He's just too shy to say so, and you haven't exactly given him or anyone else a chance."

"She likes Scott," Nicole said. "And the Valentine theme of this dance just makes it more important to be with someone you really like. There's always hope."

"I suppose." Robyn stared wistfully into space. "Jerry asked me to save the first dance for him."

"Yes, we know." Nicole rolled her eyes. "You've mentioned it a few times the past week."

"About ten times a day," Alex added. Robyn and Jerry had met at last year's school dance. They had a lot in common. Both were chronic worriers, convinced that the worst would happen in any given situation. *In fact*, Alex thought, *I've had the kind of day Robyn always expects. Anything that could wrong did go wrong.*

"I *have* to go to the mall today!" Robyn suddenly blurted out. "I saw this absolutely perfect dress last week. Of course with my luck, they're probably sold out or they won't have it in my size."

"Then we'll find something else. What's the big deal?" Nicole shrugged. "If I don't find a new outfit I really want, I'll just pull something out of my closet."

Robyn gasped. "Get real, Nicole. This is *the* social event of the school year. *I* don't want to go looking like a seventh-grade dweeb who has no sense of style. I have to get something really cool. *Today.*"

"There's still tomorrow, Robyn," Alex said. Sometimes Robyn could get a little too dramatic. "The dance doesn't start until seven-thirty."

"I can't go shopping after school tomorrow," Robyn said with a sigh. "I'm the chairperson of the decoration committee. I want to totally plaster the walls with paper hearts, and I've got about a hundred left to cut out. It's going to take forever."

Alex glanced at Robyn. She'd known about the dance decorations for a whole month, but mostly all she'd done about it was worry.

"I'm not doing anything tomorrow," Nicole said. "I'll help."

"Great!" Robyn said.

They turned onto the block where Alex had almost been run down by a Paradise Valley Chemical truck. She shuddered as she remembered being totally drenched in the goop.

"I'll be there, too." Raymond gave Robyn a thumbs-up, then looked at Alex expectantly.

"I don't know if I can. I—" Shoulders sagging, Alex let out another long, weary sigh. "I haven't finished my book report yet, and if I don't hand it in during class tomorrow, I'll have to stay after school to finish. It's either that or get an F in English."

"So you're not going to the mall with us?" Nicole asked.

"Can't. I haven't even finished reading the book yet."

"Why not?" Robyn asked. "That report was assigned over a month ago."

"I just haven't, okay?" Alex snapped again. The book report counted for a third of her English grade. Alex knew she shouldn't have put off such an important assignment until the last minute, but between her other schoolwork, her chores, Annie's schedule for studying her powers, and of course, her friends, she never seemed to have enough time to get everything done. Her parents and Annie were constantly nagging her about her tendency to procrastinate. She didn't need to be reminded by Robyn, too.

"What book did you get?" Raymond asked.

"*A Tale of Two Cities*, by Charles Dickens," Alex mumbled.

"Can't help you then," Raymond said. "I read *Moby Dick*."

"*Little Women*," Nicole said.

"I had *The Yearling*." A look of utter sadness clouded Robyn's face. "It was great until the end when—"

"I really don't want to know." Alex cut her off. She hated unhappy endings—so much so that she had stopped reading the classic Dickens story when Charles Darnay was arrested by the French revolutionary mob *again*, right after his father-in-law had saved him from the guillotine. And she had even become comfortable with the old-fashioned language of 1859. But she couldn't afford to flunk English, so she had to finish the book whether she liked it or not.

Suddenly, Alex stopped, dropped her backpack, and began to rummage through it. Raymond, Robyn, and Nicole hovered over her.

"Now what?" Nicole asked.

"The book and my notes!" Alex pulled out a bunch of loose papers, a fistful of pencils, and several dog-eared spiral notebooks. "I think I left them in my locker!"

"The school's closed, Alex," Raymond said. "It's too late to go back and get them now."

"They've got to be here!"

"Even if they are in there, you'll never find them." Robyn peered over Alex's shoulder and wrinkled her nose. "What a mess!"

Alex fumed as she dug her textbooks out of the bag. She was mad at herself for not being able to keep her work organized and even madder at Robyn for having to point it out. Then she found the tattered paperback under her looseleaf notebook. Her notes were stuffed inside it. "Whew!" she said, letting out a big breath.

"Lucky for you," Raymond said as she held it up.

"I'll say." Relieved, Alex shoved her books and papers back into the bag and stood up.

"You have to get more organized," Robyn said, opening her own backpack.

"I know, Robyn," Alex said tightly.

Robyn didn't have to search for her book report. Pulling out a file folder, she flipped it open to reveal a neat, computer-printed report. "It's not that hard to be neat, Alex. In fact, it'll make your life a whole lot easier."

"So I've heard." *From my parents, Annie, my teachers, and now you*, Alex thought with mounting irritation. *So what if I'm not a neat freak.*

"You've got to learn to manage your time,

too," Robyn went on, totally oblivious of Alex's annoyed expression.

Then Robyn held her perfectly ordered backpack under Alex's nose.

"Hey! That's *my* hat!" Alex exclaimed, spotting a familiar blue brim edged in gold. It was one of her favorites. In fact, she hadn't worn a hat to school today because she couldn't find it. *What was it doing in Robyn's backpack?*

"Oh, yeah." Robyn pulled out the cap. "You left it at my house three days ago. Bet you didn't even know it was missing, did you?" Robyn flipped the cap over her long, red hair. "And that's my point exactly."

Alex didn't care what point Robyn was trying to make. Her whole day had been a disaster, and now Robyn was making her feel like a total jerk in front of Raymond and Nicole. Alex had to take it when her parents criticized her, but she didn't have to take from Robyn.

She was getting *really* mad.

"Where are we going?" Dave asked, tightening his grip on the steering wheel.

"Back to the scene of the GC 161 accident," Vince said icily.

"Why?" Dave glanced sideways, saw Vince's chiseled jaw clench, and quickly turned his attention from the head of plant security back to the road.

"I'm hoping *something* might jog your memory." Vince stared out the windshield, his facial muscles tense with determination. "We aren't any closer to identifying that kid than we were a year and a half ago, and I'm willing to try anything. Now pay attention. The accident site is right around that corner."

"Okay, Vince." Dave wanted to find the kid as much as Vince did. Then he could go back to driving a truck and forget about working with the security chief. Vince didn't like him, and he didn't like being yelled at all the time.

Dave remembered that right before the real accident he had been fumbling with a sandwich and a soda, and he decided to recreate the events as accurately as possible. As he steered the truck around the corner, he went through the motions of trying to eat a pretend sandwich without spilling a pretend drink cup.

"What are you doing?" Vince scowled at him.

"Uh—" Dave stammered. He hadn't told Vince about the food because Vince had specifically told him *not* to stop for lunch. "Nothing, Vince."

"Well, stop it."

"Right." Sighing, Dave went through the motions in his head.

Angry and upset, Alex focused on Robyn's backpack. The neatly arranged files and books seemed to mock her own lack of organizational skills. In her mind, Alex visualized the backpack falling. She imagined Robyn's notebooks, files, and textbooks tumbling out and the book report pages flying across the street.

Then, explosively and without warning, the frustration and anger Alex had been holding in all day erupted like a volcano. Her fantasy suddenly became a powerful and uncontrollable telekinetic command that snatched Robyn's backpack from her grasp.

"What?" Robyn squealed as the bag hit the sidewalk and the orderly contents spilled out. The book report file fell open and the breeze blew the white pages away. They flew off down the block, some on the sidewalk, others in the gutter and under parked cars.

Robyn's frantic cry broke through the singular focus that had seized Alex's mind. Snapping out of it, Alex blinked, then gasped as Robyn scrambled after the flyaway book report.

What have I done? She thought frantically. She hadn't meant to mess up Robyn's books and files for *real!* Sometimes she imagined awful things she could do with her powers when people made her mad, but her fantasies had *never* actually *happened* before!

Raymond set down his books and ran to gather up the notebooks and loose papers.

"Robyn gives new meaning to the phrase 'losing your grip,'" Nicole muttered. She grabbed at a paper as it took flight, but it got away.

"I'll get it!" Raymond dashed along the grassy bank sloping upward from the sidewalk.

Alex just stared at her feet. Robyn hadn't

meant to be cruel to her. She had sincerely wanted to help Alex solve a problem that was making her life miserable. Alex realized that getting mad and striking out at her friend was unfair and mean.

And using her powers on Robyn just made it worse. Alex hadn't grabbed the backpack from Robyn with her hand. She had thrown a telekinetic tantrum and lashed out with her thoughts! It wasn't fair to treat her friend that way.

Feeling awful about everything, Alex looked up and saw Robyn darting after the book report strewn across the street. *Get in gear, Alex! You caused this mess.* She could at least help fix it instead of standing around doing nothing.

Alex automatically looked for traffic before stepping off the curb. Her breath caught in her throat when she saw a truck roaring down the street. Robyn was directly in its path, and she was so intent on picking up papers that she was completely unaware of the danger. Then Alex realized that the driver was leaning toward the man in the passenger seat and not paying attention to the road. He didn't even see Robyn!

"Robyn!" Alex yelled.

Clutching a fistful of papers, Robyn stood up and looked at Alex with a curious frown.

Frantically, Alex pointed toward the truck. "Look out!" But her warning came too late.

Robyn turned and froze in terrified surprise.

CHAPTER 2

Horrified, Alex looked back at the speeding truck. Somehow she had to save Robyn. But did she have the power to stop several tons of speeding metal with just her mind?

"Get out of the way! Move!" Nicole shouted to Robyn.

Raymond bolted down the grassy embankment. Alex knew he was reacting instinctively, hoping to reach Robyn and pull her out of harm's way. He couldn't possibly get to her before the truck did.

All of a sudden Alex got an idea. With no time

to waste or worry about getting caught using her powers, Alex reached out with her mind and telekinetically grabbed the truck's steering wheel.

Just as Alex yanked the wheel hard to the left, Robyn crouched and rolled as the truck swerved away from the curb. It barely missed hitting her and a nearby fire hydrant.

"Robyn!" Nicole screamed, then gasped. "Man-oh-man, that was close. Way too close!"

Raymond stopped to catch his breath.

Alex watched everything with a strange sense of déjà vu. She saw the plant logo on the side of the truck and realized with a jolt that it was a duplicate of the one that had almost hit her more than a year ago. And this accident had happened in exactly the same spot! Only this time no gold stuff spilled out onto the street and Alex wasn't the victim.

Robyn was, though, Alex realized, swallowing hard. *And it was all my fault.*

Please, let her be all right, Alex pleaded silently as she raced toward Robyn. The girl was sprawled on the curb a mere two feet from the stalled truck.

Dazed, Robyn sat up and shook her head as Alex reached her side. "What happened?"

"You were almost hit by a truck!" Nicole answered as she rushed up and knelt by her friend. "Are you all right?"

"I think so. Nothing seems to be broken." Robyn moved her arms and legs, testing them to be sure.

Raymond put out his hand to help Robyn to her feet.

As Alex eased back to give them room, she glanced up at the truck's cab and inhaled sharply. Dave looked down at them through the windshield. He hesitated, blinked, then opened his mouth to say something, but he didn't get a word out.

Alex recognized Vince the instant the head of plant security began to shout.

"You idiot! Can't you ever do anything right?"

"But Vince, I think—"

"Think! You don't know how to think, Dave. You don't even know how to drive!"

"But, Vince—" Turning toward Vince, Dave pointed toward the window. "I'm sure that's—"

"Come on," Vince snapped. "Let's check out those kids."

Alex heard a click as Vince pressed a button to unlock the doors. She didn't know exactly what Vince wanted to check out. Maybe he just wanted to be sure they were all right, but she couldn't afford to be wrong. She did *not* want to talk to him.

Robyn wobbled slightly as she stood up. She put her hand on the truck fender to steady herself. At the same time Alex leaned against the truck to hide her actions and sent a zapper into the electrical system under the hood. The bolt locked the doors again and jammed the mechanism.

"What was that?" Vince shouted as the locks suddenly recessed. He looked out the window with a puzzled frown.

Raymond looked at Alex. He knew what she was thinking. "Let's get out of here," Raymond said, jumping to his feet.

Vince began pounding on his locked door.

"No way!" Nicole protested. "We've got to call the police and file an accident report."

"A police report?" Robyn frowned uncertainly. "You mean press charges against the driver?"

"You have to, Robyn." Nicole was adamant. "That guy is a reckless driver. You could have been seriously hurt. We can't let him get away with this."

"I'm out of here!" Raymond headed for the sidewalk. Picking up the book report pages, Alex started after him. Insisting she was fine, Robyn hurried after them. Nicole trailed behind, then refused to leave the scene.

"Those guys almost flattened Robyn!" Nicole was furious.

"But they didn't!" Alex stuffed the book report pages into Robyn's backpack, picked it up, then grabbed her own. Even if this whole scary incident was just a bizarre coincidence, it wouldn't be smart to stick around. Dave might recognize her.

Nicole glared at her friends, then flipped open her notebook and pulled out a pen. "I'm going to get the license plate number. Somebody's got to do something about this."

Alex couldn't use her powers now to get out of this situation. Vince and the two girls would notice something as unusual as electrical bolts zapping out of nowhere or inexplicable electromagnetic force fields. Alex couldn't run away by herself, leaving the others behind, either. That would really look suspicious.

Desperate, Alex cast an anxious glance toward Raymond.

Vince had climbed halfway through the open window on the passenger side.

Raymond's eyes narrowed as he glanced toward the truck. "That's the head of plant security. Let's pound some pavement while we still can!"

"I'm with you." Robyn said, taking her backpack from Alex and slinging it over her shoulder.

"You're just going to run away?" Nicole asked incredulously.

"Right. That's exactly what we're going to do," Raymond said. "Run!"

Alex was never so glad to have a friend like

Ray. She took off after Robyn and Raymond. Now nobody could say that she didn't stand by her friends in tough times.

"Hey!" Vince yelled. "Come back here!"

Alex chanced a quick look behind her. Vince broke into a jog, then started to run. Nicole hesitated, then apparently decided she didn't want to confront Vince on her own. She charged down the sidewalk with the security man in hot pursuit and gaining.

CHAPTER 3

Alex watched as Nicole ducked to the right and disappeared into a thick stand of evergreens lining the top of the bank along the sidewalk.

Good for Nicole, Alex thought, *but not good for me*. Vince did not even glance in the direction Nicole had taken. Keeping to the sidewalk, he put on a burst of speed.

"He's getting closer!" Alex cried breathlessly.

"This way!" Raymond shouted, waving them on.

Then Alex noticed that Vince was wearing laced shoes. She might not be able to stop him, but she could slow him down again. Focusing on Vince's shoelaces, she gave the ends a telekinetic tug and untied them. Then she ran full-speed to catch up to Raymond and Robyn.

As they rounded the corner at the end of the block, Raymond darted to the right and bounded over the embankment. Alex did not risk looking back again as she followed him and Robyn down the other side, through a tangle of leafless brush and evergreens, then behind a rocky outcropping. Nicole was a few yards away, catching up to them.

"Is he still behind us?" Alex paused to drink in great gulps of air. It was a struggle to keep herself from collapsing on the ground—her legs were shaking like wet noodles.

"We lost him," Nicole said casually. "I watched him from the trees when I realized he wasn't following me. No wonder you didn't want to stick around, Ray. That was Vince!"

"You know Vince?" Raymond asked.

"I worked for him on Career Day last year, remember?" Nicole said. "What a weird guy! Really intense and suspicious. He didn't look so tough today, though. His shoelaces came untied and he tripped over his own feet when you guys went around the corner. He turned back."

"Yes!" Alex whispered, then sank onto a fallen tree trunk. She didn't think she could run another step.

"Lucky for us," Robyn said as she sat down beside Alex.

"Yeah. Real lucky." Raymond glanced at Alex and grinned when she shrugged.

At least something went right today, Alex thought.

"We can still nail them, though." Nicole tapped her notebook. "I got the license plate number, and we know Vince was in the truck."

"Forget it." Robyn held up her hands. "I wasn't hurt, and there wasn't really an accident. It would be totally insane to make trouble with Danielle Atron over nothing."

Alex nodded. As chief executive officer of Paradise Valley Chemical, Danielle Atron was not just in charge of the plant, she was a powerful force in the town. Nobody messed with her.

"Reckless driving and endangerment is *not*

nothing," Nicole insisted. "Those guys drive plant trucks all over town. There was an accident on that same street just last year. The plant hushed it up, though, and right after that Danielle Atron's security guys were going to everyone's house with some weird handprint gizmo."

"They were?" Robyn seemed surprised. "Why?"

Nicole lowered her voice. "Nobody knows."

"They didn't come to my house," Robyn said.

"They didn't?" Alex asked. "Are you sure?"

"Positive. I think I'd remember if a bunch of plant police showed up at my door with a mysterious device." Robyn shuddered. "Kinda creepy, huh?"

"Yeah," Alex mumbled. She had destroyed the handprint ID device with a zap to protect herself. Obviously, Vince and Dave hadn't been to Robyn's home before that happened.

"Super-suspicious, if you ask me," Nicole said with rising indignation. "But everyone's so intimidated by Danielle Atron, no one ever questions anything she does. It's not right."

"I know," Robyn said with a weary sigh. "But since nothing really bad happened, it's not worth it to risk making her angry. There's no telling what she might do!"

"Robyn's right about that," Alex agreed. "Better to just forget the whole thing."

Danielle Atron had lots of power in town, and over everyone in it. It wasn't fair, but that's the way it was. Alex had her own reasons for not wanting to pursue the matter, but she couldn't confide in Nicole. It was just lucky for her that Robyn wasn't interested in taking any chances with the CEO, either.

"I'm with Alex," Raymond added for good measure.

"End of discussion," Robyn said, setting her backpack on the ground. She began to sort through the crumpled papers.

Defeated by a vote of three to one, Nicole grudgingly surrendered. "Okay, okay," she grumbled. "I think it's a shame to pass up such a perfect opportunity to show Danielle Atron that she can't bully everyone, but if that's what you guys want to do—"

"Rats!" Robyn flipped through the pages on her lap again.

"I said okay! I'll drop it," Nicole replied.

"No, that's not the problem," Robyn said.

"I'll say." Raymond eyed the papers in Robyn's lap. "You won't be able to hand in that book report. It's all torn and dirty. You can't very well say it was run over by a truck."

"Yeah, and a page is missing." Carefully returning the papers to her backpack, Robyn stood up. "No problem. I can print out another copy. The file is still on the computer."

"You two coming to the mall with us?" Nicole asked as she and Robyn started to leave.

"Naw." Raymond shook his head. "Louis is home with that flu thing, and I've got to drop off his assignments. I can save five minutes if I cut through this new development." He gestured toward a row of houses under construction.

"I've got to get to work on my book report," Alex said. "Guess I'll go with Ray. I can use the extra five minutes."

"Catch ya later then." Robyn waved.

Alex overheard Robyn talking to Nicole as the two girls left in the opposite direction.

"I just hope there's time to get to the mall after

I'm done printing a new report," Robyn said. "Half the afternoon is gone already."

"Will you stop worrying," Nicole said.

"What if my book report file got erased somehow?" Robyn moaned. "I'll have to type it in again, and we'll *never* get to the mall."

Another thing to feel guilty about, Alex realized. *I should have stayed in bed*, she thought glumly.

Vince stalked back to the truck. He was furious with himself for stumbling over his own shoelaces and letting a bunch of kids outrun him. It was getting harder and harder to cope with the humiliating fact that the GC 161 kid had managed to elude him for more than a year. Sooner or later Danielle Atron would get fed up with his failures and hire someone else to do the job. Plus he did not want to tell Danielle Atron that Dave had almost run down another kid. Although the CEO had enough clout in Paradise Valley to pacify the police and prevent charges from being filed, arranging it was a hassle. By running away, the kids had actually saved him a lot of trouble.

Finding Dave relaxing against the truck with his eyes closed just made Vince angrier. "This is no time for a nap, Dave!"

Dave's eyes popped open. "Did you catch them?"

"No, I didn't catch them. I don't even know why I was trying to!" Vince glared at Dave.

"But that was the kid, Vince! That was her!"

The uncharacteristic intensity in Dave's voice and expression gave Vince pause. Dave was normally oblivious about why it was so important to find the GC 161 kid. In the words of the local teens, Dave lived in a perpetual state of *no-duh*. It was unlikely that he had almost hit the *same* kid in the same spot, but Vince had to consider every possibility no matter how improbable.

"Okay, Dave. Get back in the truck," Vince said levelly. Taking a deep breath, he forced himself to calm down. "They can't have gotten far. If we find out where she lives, we can find out who she is."

"A couple of them looked familiar." Dave squinted as though that would improve his thinking abilities. "Alvarez? Avocado?"

"Alvarado." Vince frowned. "And what's-his-name's daughter. Greg Muck or something like that."

"Why don't we just ask them about their friend?"

"Brilliant, Dave," Vince said sarcastically. "If we start questioning her friends, they'll get suspicious and warn her. Besides, I'm not convinced it's the same kid."

Gritting his teeth, Vince gave Dave a boost back through the window, then hauled himself through the small opening. He winced as Dave started the truck, backed it up a few feet, then drove forward to make a U-turn. He missed hitting the fire hydrant by a couple of inches. Once they were headed in the right direction, Vince scanned the streets and yards while he listened.

"I'm almost positive it's the same kid," Dave said excitedly. "I was leaning over just like the last time . . ." Dave caught himself before he blurted out that he had leaned over to pick up the sandwich he had dropped. "Anyway, when I looked up and saw a kid wearing a hat, and standing in the middle of the road in front of me *today*, it was like instant replay."

"*Instant* replay?" Vince rolled his eyes. "It's been a year and a half."

A bewildered frown passed across Dave's face, then he shrugged. "Yeah. The whole thing just flashed before my eyes. The kid diving out of the way. The truck hitting the curb. I missed the fire hydrant, though."

"Twice. Thank you." Sighing, Vince ran his hand over the bristle of his short hair. "I admit it's an unbelievable coincidence that everything then and now happened exactly the same way, but—"

"Not exactly *exactly* the same way, Vince. I didn't run the truck into the curb this time like I did last time."

"Well, who do you think did it?" Vince said tightly. "*You* were driving."

"Yes, I was," Dave admitted. "Right up until the point when the wheel just turned by itself. *I* didn't do it." Raising his right hand, Dave looked Vince in the eye. "Honest."

"Watch the road," Vince growled, frustration

twisting his stomach. "Steering wheels don't turn by themselves."

"Oh, right." Dave frowned thoughtfully. "There must be something wrong with the truck."

"A logical conclusion," Vince said sarcastically.

"But I'm sure it was the same kid," Dave said again.

Although Vince desperately wanted to have the whole miserable GC 161 business settled, he didn't trust Dave's faulty memory or observations. Danielle Atron's hopes of finding the kid had been raised too many times without results.

"Okay, Dave. Let's assume it's the same kid. *This* time you'll recognize her when you see her again, right?"

"Maybe. It all happened so fast—"

Vince had heard that excuse at least a hundred times. As he opened his mouth to shout, Dave pulled a dirty white paper off the dashboard and handed it to him. "What's this?" Vince asked.

"The kid dropped it. I found it under the truck."

As Vince looked at the computer-printed page, a satisfied grin spread across his face. His mind was hatching up a plan, a foolproof plan. "Go back to the plant, Dave."

"But we'll lose her again!"

"The plant, Dave. I've got things to do before our five o'clock meeting with Ms. Atron. I don't want to be late."

"Me neither." Dave turned right to take a shortcut back to Paradise Valley Chemical. "Are we in trouble again?"

"No. She just wants to brief us on another undercover surveillance opportunity at the junior high school."

"At least we have some good news for her."

"No, we don't," Vince said sharply. "We're not going to say anything about this kid until we have positive proof that she's the one we've been looking for. Got it?"

"Yeah." Grumbling, Dave slouched over the wheel.

"Don't forget it." Vince had to be sure before he hauled a kid into the lab to be scanned for GC 161. They'd have to make up a terrible story about the kid's life being in danger to justify their actions. Bringing in the *wrong* kid would prompt questions from parents and friends, questions Danielle Atron would not want to answer.

Better to watch and wait, Vince thought. He'd gather his evidence slowly and methodically, beginning with the girl's name. It wasn't on the page, but it wouldn't be hard to match the printing font and page setup to a report in the same format.

Vince would have the kid when he found out who turned in a book report on *The Yearling*.

CHAPTER 4

Raymond jumped a low hedge and landed on the sidewalk. "We haven't had this much excitement in a long time," he said. "I've kinda missed it."

"Not me." Alex pushed through the hedge and fell into step beside him. "Always wondering when and where Vince and Dave are gonna pop up next can drive a person crazy."

"Ah, come on, Alex. It's not that bad."

"Easy for you to say, Ray," Alex said a little testily. "You can go anywhere and do anything you want without worrying about ending up as a top secret project in Danielle Atron's lab. But I can't, and it's starting to bum me out."

"Yeah, I guess it is, isn't it?" Raymond sighed sympathetically. "Your powers are so cool, sometimes I forget about what you have to deal with because you've got them. Sorry."

"No, Ray. I'm the one who's sorry—again. You're always there when I need you, like today. I shouldn't get upset with you just because things are not going great for me."

"Forget it, Alex. We all have bad days, and you do have a radical problem."

"At least *you* understand that." Shaking her head, Alex shuffled around the corner of the block as though she carried the weight of the world on her shoulders. "That's still no excuse for losing my temper, but I can apologize to you. Robyn doesn't have a clue."

"Robyn?" Raymond frowned uncertainly.

"I *made* her backpack fall, Ray. I didn't mean to. I really didn't," Alex said anxiously. "I was just thinking about how mad I was at her, and *wham!* The next thing I know the pack's on the ground and Robyn's almost turned into a pancake by that truck."

"You mean it just happened on its own?" Raymond's eyes widened and he drew back slightly. "You didn't deliberately reach out with your mind and grab her bag?"

"Don't worry. It's never happened before, and it *won't* happen again. I promise."

"I hope not, although I can think of a few people who actually deserve a touch of the old Alex Mack whammy. Like those two guys." Raymond nodded toward the intersection just ahead.

Alex stopped short as she saw what Raymond meant. It was the Paradise Valley Chemical truck. "Won't they ever give up?" she wailed.

As the truck stopped at the four corners, Alex braced himself to run again. Dave looked right at her, but then he drove on.

"Huh. That's funny," Raymond said.

Alex had a thought. "Hey! Maybe Dave didn't recognize me, Ray. I thought he had when he almost hit Robyn, and that's why Vince was chasing us, but maybe not!"

"He sure tried hard enough to catch us," Raymond said.

Alex shrugged. "Could be he just wanted to make sure Robyn was all right. Danielle Atron *is* his boss. Who would want to tell her that Dave had another accident on the same street?"

"Except nothing terrible happened to Robyn. She got scared, but she didn't get run over or doused with a dangerous chemical."

"No thanks to me." Alex's sense of relief for her friend was dampened by feelings of guilt.

"Robyn doesn't know that."

"No, but I do." Alex set her jaw. Somehow, she had to square things with Robyn. "Robyn was absolutely right about everything she said, Ray. I *am* disorganized, and if I was honest with myself, I'd face the fact that Scott only likes me as a friend. I can't apologize to Robyn for messing up her stuff, but I can take her advice."

"Great!" Raymond stopped in front of Louis's house. "Having a good time never hurt anyone."

"A good time?"

"Yeah. If you don't stand on the sidelines

mooning over Scott, you'll have a blast at the dance."

"I wasn't talking about going to the dance, Ray. I'm going home to get organized and work on my book report."

"Oh." Obviously disappointed, Raymond sighed. "So you're definitely not going to the dance?"

"No, I just haven't decided." Waving to Raymond, Alex headed for her house. She really didn't want to miss the dance, but it wouldn't be any fun if she was uncomfortable all night. Alex just couldn't watch Scott dance with Kelly the whole time. It would just be too humiliating.

"Alex!" Annie hollered up the stairs. "Phone!"

"Coming!" Placing her book face-down on the bed, Alex ran to her parents' room to take the call.

Although she was determined to hand in her report during class, Alex welcomed any excuse to stop reading. The young, handsome, and kind Charles Darnay had been sentenced to having his head chopped off. But he wasn't guilty! His dead father and uncle had committed the terrible crimes, but the French revolutionaries didn't care. They just wanted revenge.

Belly flopping onto her parents' bed, Alex lifted the receiver, then rolled onto her back. "Hello."

"Hey, Alex. This is Scott."

Alex sat bolt upright. "Hi, Scott."

"Sorry to bother you, but I thought you might be able to help me out."

"Sure. Glad to. What's up?" Alex hoped he couldn't hear that she was practically hyperventilating.

"I'm the chairperson of the refreshment committee for the dance, and I'm short a bunch of brownies. Could you bring some tomorrow night?"

"I would, but I'm not going—" Biting her lip, Alex pounded her fist on the bed. *What a totally stupid thing to say! Scott asks for a favor, and I turn him down!*

"Oh, that's too bad," Scott said sincerely. "Yeah, there's this flu going around. Kelly had to leave school early today because she came down with it, too. That's why I'm calling. She was supposed to bring the brownies, but now she can't go."

Kelly wasn't going to the dance!

"I'm not sick," Alex said quickly. "I, uh—" *Think, Alex!* She didn't want Scott to know the *real* reason she wasn't going, so she blurted out the first excuse that came to mind. "My parents are busy and I don't have a ride." *Oh no*, she thought, biting her knuckle. *Now he'll think I don't have any friends.*

"Well, that's not a problem," Scott said. "I'm sure my Dad won't mind swinging by to pick you up."

"Really? Great? How many?"

"How many?" Scott asked.

"How many brownies?" Alex slapped her forehead. *I sound like a stuttering chipmunk!*

"Three dozen ought to do it, if it's not too much trouble."

"It's not," Alex assured him.

"See you around seven-fifteen then. And thanks, Alex."

After Scott hung up, Alex clutched the receiver to her chest. She didn't move for a few seconds, and then the unbelievable meaning of the conversation hit her.

She was going to the dance with Scott!

Whooping with joy, Alex hung up the phone. She was so excited she thought she was going to burst. She began to bounce on the bed, throwing a pillow up in the air. She sat back and let the pillow land on her face, then screamed into it so no one would hear.

"I assume you can explain this childish display." Annie paused in the doorway and raised an eyebrow.

Alex removed the pillow and burst out laughing.

Annie frowned. "This isn't some kind of delayed reaction to GC 161 or something, is it?"

"No way," Alex said breathlessly.

"Then what gives?"

"I'm going to the Valentine's dance with Scott!" Alex jumped off the bed and dashed past Annie.

Annie followed Alex back to their room. "So Scott finally asked you for a date."

"It's not a date exactly." Alex threw open the

closet door and began pushing hangers back and forth on the rod. She pulled out a red velour dress with gold buttons, then a long, off-white tunic with full, cuffed sleeves that she wore with black tights. Tossing both outfits on her bed, she stepped back to study them.

"If it's not a date, then what is it?" Annie asked.

"He's giving me a ride." Alex avoided Annie's gaze.

"That's not the same thing as *going* with him, Alex."

Alex knew that, but she wasn't going to let that minor detail spoil an unexpected high point in an otherwise dismal day. Since Kelly wasn't going, Scott didn't *have* a date. He had asked her to dance before, and Alex was sure he would again. Maybe more than once. And they'd be arriving at the dance together!

But not in one of these outfits, Alex quickly decided. She couldn't possibly wear *anything* she had in her closet. This was the chance she'd been dreaming of, and nothing less than something new, cool, and totally *now* would do.

"I've got to go to the mall."

"You've got to finish your book report." Annie picked up the paperback lying on Alex's bed.

"I will. Later."

"Right." Annie thumbed through the pages and smiled. *"A Tale of Two Cities.* Great book. I loved it."

"Figures," Alex muttered as she rummaged through her top drawer searching for her red beret. Scott had called just as Alex finished reading Charles Darnay's last letter to his beautiful wife, Lucie. The Bastille was an inescapable prison, and with less than thirty pages to go, Alex was certain poor Charles was doomed. She'd deal with that tragedy later. Right now she just wanted to enjoy being happy.

"Don't expect me to help you with the report," Annie added. "You're on your own, remember?"

"How could I forget? But don't worry. I'll get it done even if I have to stay up all night."

Running downstairs, Alex dialed Robyn's house. Robyn's mother told her that Robyn and Nicole had left for the mall a few minutes before. Just as she was hanging up, Alex heard her father's car pull into the drive. She grabbed her backpack and rushed outside.

"Dad!" Opening the passenger door, Alex slid into the front seat before he turned off the engine.

"Hey, Alex." George Mack smiled warmly. "So glad to see me you couldn't wait until I came inside, huh?"

"I've *got* to go the mall. It's really important. Will you take me?" Alex gave her dad her best I'm-desperate-and-nobody-else-can-help-me look. "Please?"

"Sure, but what about dinner?"

"I'll fix something for myself later."

Relaxing as Mr. Mack shifted into reverse and pulled back into the street, Alex forgot all about the bad luck and frustrating disasters that had plagued her all day.

She was going to the dance with Scott.

Nothing else could possibly go wrong now.

CHAPTER 5

"Cheer up, Vince." Pausing before the automatic doors leading into Paradise Valley Mall, Dave gently slapped Vince on the back. "This'll be fun."

"It's not supposed to be fun." Vince swatted Dave's hand away. "It's work, Dave. Work! Ms. Atron is paying Steel Wool double their usual fee to play at the dance so we can infiltrate and look for the GC 161 kid." Vince and Dave would be undercover working the lights and the sound board.

"I thought you weren't going to tell her that we found the kid?"

"I didn't, you dolt!" Vince snapped. "Ms. Atron doesn't know we have a specific suspect. Remember that."

"Right." Dave nodded, then sagged. "Too bad we aren't going to play in the band, though." As a little kid, he had driven his mother nuts banging on pots and pans, and he still dreamed of playing drums in a real rock band.

Vince and Dave stepped aside as a large group of kids surged through the sliding doors into the parking lot. Shaking his head, Vince stalked through the automatic doors into the mall.

"Sure is crowded," Dave said as he followed Vince through the swarm of high-spirited teens filling the wide main aisle.

"Exactly," Vince said. "So keep your eyes open. Looks like every kid in town is here. If we spot that girl tonight, we'll save ourselves some time and trouble tomorrow."

As they walked by Fashion Express, Dave paused. "Let's go in this store, Vince."

"Did you see her?" Vince asked expectantly.

"No, but Fashion Express has some really neat

stuff, and I want to get something to wear to-morrow night."

"Give me a break. We are not here to shop, Dave."

Dave never argued with Vince, but he wished Vince knew that he was hoping the band would let him play drums for one song. Just in case the band agreed, he wanted to *look* like a rock and roll drummer, not a truck driver.

"Band roadies don't wear suits, Vince," Dave persisted.

Vince frowned thoughtfully.

"And *all* the kids shop here," Dave added for good measure.

Vince turned toward the doors. "I guess this is as good a place to start looking as any."

Grinning, Dave charged past Vince into the clothing store.

Alex impatiently wove her way through the crowd. She was anxious to find Robyn and Nicole to tell them about Scott, but the mall was a mob scene. It looked like every kid in town who didn't have the flu was shopping for the dance.

"Oops, sorry." A girl with long blond hair bumped Alex as she tried to edge by in the crush. "Hey, Alex!"

"Hi, Rhonda! How's it going?" Alex grinned and stepped back against the display window before they both got trampled.

"Fabulously," Rhonda gushed. "I found this absolutely terrific dress for the dance tomorrow night. If you're looking for something to wear, check out Teen Scene. They are stocked to the ceiling with gorgeous stuff."

"Thanks. I will. I've got to find something tonight because I'm hoping to help decorate after school tomorrow if I finish my report in time. And Scott's picking me up at seven-fifteen."

"Scott? The ninth-grade hunk with the gorgeous eyes? That Scott?" Rhonda was totally impressed.

Reality struck Alex like a lightning bolt. Rhonda had misinterpreted her words and thought she was going as Scott's date. That wasn't true, and she had to say so.

"He's just giving me a ride."

"Cool! My parents are dropping me off."

Rhonda rolled her eyes. "I've got to run. We'll talk tomorrow, okay?"

"See ya then." Alex's shoulders drooped as she shuffled toward Fashion Express. She was feeling like a popped balloon. Even though Rhonda thought getting a ride with Scott was cool, the conversation had forced Alex to face facts. A ride was just a ride. Making a big deal out of Scott's friendly gesture was foolish and immature.

"Hey! There's Alex!"

Alex looked up and saw Nicole wave, then nudge Robyn. Separating herself from the crowd, Alex joined them at the front of the store. "Thought I'd find you two here."

"Well, we sure didn't expect to see you," Robyn said. "Did you finish your book report already?"

"No," Alex admitted, "but I've got all my notes organized and I'm almost done with the book. So I decided to take a break and meet you. Besides, I've decided to go the dance and I don't have anything to wear."

"What made you change your mind?" Robyn asked.

"Well, I just couldn't say no when Scott called to ask me—"

"Scott asked you to the dance?" Nicole's eyes widened.

"I thought he was going with Kelly," Robyn said.

"He was, but Kelly got sick and can't—"

"So he asked you!" Nicole gave her a thumbs up. "Way to go, Alex!"

"It's about time!" Robyn smiled. "I guess persistence really does pay off."

"No, he just asked me to bring—" Alex desperately tried to explain, but they were too excited and distracted to listen.

"Come on," Robyn said as she moved toward the store entrance. "I've just got to find out if my dress is still here."

"But—" Alex threw up her hands in exasperation as Robyn and Nicole rushed into Fashion Express. She had to tell them Scott was just giving her a ride, but obviously that wasn't going to be possible until they had finished their shopping and calmed down.

Alex hesitated as she stepped inside the door. Fashion Express was one of the two really *in* clothing stores that catered to boys and girls, and it was as busy as the rest of the mall. Robyn and Nicole had disappeared in the throng of teenagers wandering through a maze of towering partitions.

Walking down the center aisle, Alex scanned the narrow side aisles looking for the girls and keeping an eye out for an outfit, too. As long as she was going to the dance, she might as well look her best. She didn't have anything particular in mind, except that it had to be better than anything she had *ever* worn before.

An outfit arranged on the far wall captured her attention. The blue and white print skirt matched with a white knit top and blue denim vest was a definite possibility. Alex turned down a long aisle formed by high partitions full of shirts, hats, vests, and jeans. She almost bumped into the two men looking through an assortment of vests before she realized they were Vince and Dave.

Executing an abrupt about-face, Alex quickly retreated to a break in the rack and ducked into it. Startled and breathless, she paused in the space separating vests and jackets to calm her wildly beating heart. *What are they doing here?* She knew they couldn't possibly be shopping for clothes. Funky T-shirts, flashy vests, and jeans were *not* Vince's style.

"Yes, Dave," she heard Vince say. "You can go back to driving a truck," Vince raised his voice in irritation, "*after* we have a positive ID!"

Clamping her hand over her mouth to muffle a gasp, Alex peeked around the hanging vests and strained to hear.

"Maybe by Monday, huh, Vince?"

"That all depends. We don't even know her name, yet."

Alex was not surprised that Vince didn't recall her name, even though they had met more than once. He never remembered her father's name correctly, either.

"If you were absolutely *certain* that was the same kid we saw today," Vince continued, "I

57

wouldn't hesitate to make a move. But you're not, so we have to be cautious."

"I'm pretty sure. Whoa! I like this one!" Dave held up a blue vest with a swirling design stitched in gold thread.

Alex's mind reeled. Vince and Dave were not just trying to identify an unknown kid anymore. They were in the mall looking for *her!*

"Pretty sure isn't good enough," Vince mumbled. "We're getting close, but I need positive proof." Vince pulled a black leather vest off the rack and rubbed his chin as he studied it.

Too close! Alex had to lose them—and fast. She decided to risk walking casually back down the aisle while their attention was on the vests. Taking a deep breath, she quietly stepped out of hiding.

"There she is!" Robyn called out behind her.

Oh, no! Alex froze in her tracks. *I'll never get out of this one!*

CHAPTER 6

Alex glanced back and saw Robyn and Nicole standing at the other end of the aisle. Vince and Dave looked toward the two girls, who hesitated and stared back at them uncertainly. Robyn's hand was still raised in a wave intended to attract Alex's attention.

Alex recovered first. She needed a diversion to escape the store before the plant security men noticed her. Concentrating with her mind, she telekinetically shifted several stacks of hats to the edge of a high shelf directly above the two men, then gave the stacks an extra mental nudge. The hats suddenly toppled down on Vince and Dave.

Vince dropped to the floor, throwing his hands over his head to protect himself from falling felt, canvas, and leather headgear. Dave ducked.

Robyn and Nicole stared in open-mouthed astonishment, then doubled over laughing.

Moving backward in the opposite direction, Alex waved frantically. She couldn't shout at them for fear of alerting Vince and Dave. When Robyn finally looked up and met her gaze, Alex gestured toward the exit.

Nodding, Robyn tugged on Nicole's sleeve. As they darted down the aisle, Alex turned and walked quickly toward the other end of the display partition.

"Hey, Vince." Dave said loudly. "That's her!"

Determined not to panic, Alex walked a little faster and didn't look back. She was brought to a halt when a sales clerk suddenly appeared in front of her.

"What's going on here?" the woman demanded.

"Uh—" Flustered by the unexpected and dangerous delay, Alex stared at the frowning clerk.

Then she had a sudden brainstorm. "A shelf broke or something. Ask those guys." Alex made a thumbing gesture over her shoulder.

"Oh, my." Forgetting Alex, the woman scurried toward Vince and Dave. "Are you all right? Here, let me help you with those."

"We're fine!" Vince barked and rose out from under a pile of hats, protesting as the worried clerk fussed over him.

Alex bolted for the exit as fast as her legs could carry her.

Robyn and Nicole were pacing in front of the doors outside the store. Expecting Vince and Dave to rush out any second to follow her, Alex kept walking fast when her friends sprang toward her.

"Those aren't the same guys that almost ran me down today, were they?" Robyn asked as she caught up to Alex.

"That was them, Robyn," Nicole insisted, easing in between the two girls. "Vince and that goofy guy he's always hanging out with. The head of plant security is not someone you forget!

Especially after you've been one of his recruits for a day."

"It was them," Alex agreed, breathing a little easier as the crowd closed in around them. She glanced over her shoulder, but Vince and Dave were nowhere in sight.

"And you thought *you* were having a bad day, Alex." Robyn chuckled. "Talk about accidents waiting to happen! Those guys are majorly dangerous!"

"To themselves," Nicole grinned. "Between his partner's lousy driving, his own shoelaces, and a pile of kamikaze hats, this has not been one of the mighty Vince's better days."

"Now there's an understatement," Robyn went on.

Alex only nodded. Robyn and Nicole didn't have any idea how dangerous Vince and Dave really were or that she was responsible for all their bad luck that day. What she really wanted to do was run like a screaming maniac from the mall, but instead she made every effort to appear casual.

"Anybody who attracts disaster like this Vince

person should have a warning sign pinned to him," Nicole said. "I mean, it's like those hats were just sitting on that shelf *waiting* for those guys to walk by."

"Maybe it was cosmic justice because they almost hit Robyn with a truck this afternoon," Alex said brightly. She relaxed when Robyn and Nicole laughed. Neither one seemed to think there was anything unusual about the incident.

"But what were they doing in Fashion Express?" Nicole's dark eyes narrowed with suspicion.

"Shopping," Robyn said. "This *is* the only mall in town."

"Vince may be a tough guy, but he doesn't strike me as the leather and denim type," Nicole said pointedly.

Alex knew that Nicole was like a bulldog with a bone when her mind latched onto a disturbing problem. She didn't let go unless something more appealing was dangled in front of her.

"Speaking of shopping," Alex said. "Let's get moving, okay? It's after seven, and we're running out of time."

"Thank you, Alex. As I suspected, Fashion Express was completely sold out of the dress I liked." Sighing heavily, Robyn lapsed back into her usual, fatalistic attitude. "I seriously doubt I'll find anything else that complements my coloring so perfectly. Being a redhead is a major disadvantage sometimes."

"Rhonda found a nice dress at Teen Scene," Alex said.

"Really?" Robyn cocked her head to consider it, then turned toward the escalator to the second level. "Then I guess we'd better check it out."

After scouring the aisles of Teen Scene and trying on a dozen various styles, Alex headed to Threads, a vintage clothing boutique where she finally found a dress she really liked. Checking out her reflection in a full-length mirror, she was delightfully amazed. Made of smokey blue velvet with a darker blue bodice and tiny beads around the neckline, the dress made her feel like she wasn't a total teenage dweeb after all.

"I can't believe what that dress does for you, Alex," Robyn said. "It makes you look sixteen— easy. Scott will absolutely *melt* when he sees you."

"About Scott . . ." Alex hesitated, then blurted out the truth. They had all been so busy trying things on that she hadn't had an opportunity before. "I'm not exactly *going* to the dance with him. He just called to ask if I'd bring brownies because Kelly can't, and then he offered me a ride when I told him I didn't have one."

Robyn and Nicole just stared at her for a moment.

Embarrassed, Alex lowered her gaze.

"Well, that's something," Robyn said. "Scott could have called anyone in school to bring brownies, but he didn't. He called you."

Alex looked up at Robyn gratefully. Instead of saying, "I told you so," Robyn was being supportive and encouraging.

"Robyn's got a point there, Alex," Nicole said. "He didn't have to offer you a ride, either."

"Scott was just being nice, Nicole. He didn't want me to miss the dance just because I didn't have a ride, so he offered to bring me. But it's only a ride."

"Maybe. Maybe not," Robyn said, draping a comforting arm over Alex's shoulder. "Driving to the dance with him *does* give you a certain advantage. You'll have a ten-minute head start on everyone else for getting his attention."

"Yeah, right." Alex shook her head despairingly. "It'll probably take me that long just to get over being tongue-tied. I mean, I'm not exactly a whiz at snappy dialogue under normal circumstances. Plus, talking to Scott with his father listening will *not* be like having a casual conversation at school."

"So don't talk." Pausing, Nicole set the black skirt, white blouse, and red vest she had chosen aside.

"So what am I supposed to do?" Alex asked.

Nicole gathered the hair that fell over Alex's ears and pulled the long strands up high on her head. "I say, dazzle him with your good looks." Her friend leaned back to study the effect of the makeshift hairdo. "If you do your hair up like this and I loan you my silver choker, you'll look absolutely—"

"Elegant," Robyn said.

"Stunning," Nicole agreed. "Scott will be totally blown away."

"Do you really think so?" Alex asked.

Robyn shrugged. "It could happen."

"Buy the dress, Alex."

After making their purchases, Alex led the way toward the escalator. Her spirits soared in spite of her worries. Maybe Scott really would notice! Maybe when he picked her up tomorrow night, he'd be so overwhelmed he'd forget he had only offered her a ride and instead he'd actually spend time with her at the dance. Like they were together. It *could* happen. . . .

"Watch it, Alex!" Nicole grabbed her arm to keep her from running into a bench.

"Thanks. Guess I'm a little preoccupied."

"A little?" Nicole raised an eyebrow.

Robyn opened her bag and looked inside. "I'm not sure I should have bought this dress. It's not forest green."

"No, it's not. But it's a much better shade for you," Alex said sincerely. Robyn would look super in the flowing, flower-print dress that combined several muted green hues. The long, attached vest laced up the front and was a darker, solid green that looked great with her red hair.

"You *both* worry too much," Nicole observed as she stepped onto the down escalator.

Alex and Robyn scooted onto the step behind her.

"I don't believe it," Nicole said, shaking her head. "There they are again!"

Alex looked across the fountain to see Vince and Dave on the up escalator. Dave fumbled with two shopping bags, then looked up. His eyes widened, and Alex knew he had seen them.

"What is with those guys?" Robyn exclaimed.

"I don't know," Nicole said, "but they must be running down the up escalator for a reason."

Yeah, Alex thought desperately. *They don't want to lose track of me again.*

Heart thumping and stricken with anxiety, Alex felt a warm, pulsing sensation prickle her skin. She was starting to glow, which she tended to do when she started freaking about something, and there was no place to hide! Except behind Robyn.

Alex ducked, then realized that hiding wasn't

enough. If Vince and Dave reached the lower level first, they could cut off her escape route.

Thrown off balance by Alex's sudden drop beside her, Robyn reached out and grabbed the escalator handgrip. At the same instant, Alex sent a zapper into the metal wall and through the wiring. She wasn't worried about the zapper being seen or shocking anyone. Her body hid the flash and the steps and siderails of the escalator were covered with rubber. The electrical bolt sped into the motor driving both sets of escalators, speeding up the mechanisms.

Squealing with surprise at the sudden increase in speed, Robyn braced herself as the down escalator zoomed them to the lower level.

"Whoa!" Nicole laughed and jumped off at the bottom with Alex and Robyn right behind her. "That was more fun than the super slide at Luna Park!"

Stumbling slightly because of her crouched position, Alex let the forward momentum carry her into the crowd. As she righted herself, she heard everyone around her laughing. Looking back toward the escalators, Alex couldn't help smiling, too.

Still trying to run down the up escalator, Vince and Dave were virtually running in place. The stairs were moving upward as fast as they were moving down.

"Well, I gotta say one thing for those guys," Nicole giggled. "They're not lazy. Maybe they're trying to get a free workout here instead of joining the gym."

Noticing a maintenance man rushing toward the malfunctioning escalator, Alex edged back. "Come on. I've got to get home and finish my book report."

"And I've got to study for a history test," Nicole said.

"I'm going to bed." Robyn clutched her shopping bag close to her chest. "This whole day has been exhausting. First I almost get run over by a truck, and then we get chased. And I have never been on an escalator that did *that* before!"

"Me, neither," Nicole said, "but it's a perfect example of what can go wrong when a construction project is given to the lowest bidder. And the innocent public are the ones who have to suffer."

Alex followed Nicole's gaze as she glanced back. Vince and Dave staggered off the escalator as it ground to a stop.

"Or maybe those guys are jinxed," Nicole said.

"I don't know about that, Nicole," Robyn said seriously, "but they're sure starting to get on my nerves."

Alex could relate to that. At least Robyn didn't have to live with the constant fear that Vince and Dave would always be lurking about in their relentless quest to find the GC 161 accident victim.

"Too weird," Nicole muttered.

"Creepy." Robyn shuddered.

"Yeah," Alex sighed. Robyn and Nicole were not stupid. Sooner or later they'd realize that a lot of weird stuff happened when they were with her. Someday, somehow, they'd find out she had special powers and a problem with the CEO of Paradise Valley Chemical. Whether they figured it out on their own or she told them, Alex didn't think they'd be thrilled about being left out for so long. They usually told each other everything. But according to Annie, everyone's safety depended on keeping the secret. Danielle Atron could make life miserable for anyone she suspected of withholding information, too.

What Robyn and Nicole *didn't* know wouldn't hurt them.

CHAPTER 7

"Hey, Alex! Wake up."

"Huh?" Alex opened her eyes to find Raymond staring at her. Her chin was resting on her crossed arms, and her lunch sat untouched on the cafeteria table. Sitting up with a quick shake of her head, she blinked to clear her blurred vision. "Hi, Ray."

"Having another rotten day?" Raymond swung one long leg over the bench and settled beside her.

"No, not really." Alex yawned and stretched.

"I was up most of the night finishing my book report. Got it done, though."

"Nice going. You deserve a prize for getting through that book. A story about a couple of cities sounds pretty boring."

"Actually, it wasn't boring, Raymond. For a while I couldn't read anymore because I was so sure Charles Darnay was going to die. I mean, there just didn't seem to be any way out, you know? But then I had to keep reading to find out what would happen."

"He escaped though, huh?"

"Yeah." Alex's eyes started to mist just thinking about the ending. "He had this friend, Sidney Carton, who looked just like him. Sidney went to visit Charles in prison right before they were going to haul him off to the guillotine. Sidney drugged him, switched clothes, and took his place in the prison so this spy he blackmailed could get Charles out."

"Wait a minute. Sidney *volunteered* to be decapitated instead of the other guy?" Raymond sat back with a skeptical look. "Why would anyone do anything so stupid?"

"It wasn't stupid." Alex sighed, still astounded at the enormous impact the book had had on her. "Sidney hadn't lived a very productive life, and he secretly loved Charles Darnay's wife, Lucie. If Charles had died, Lucie's life would have been ruined, too, and Sidney wanted her to be happy. By sacrificing himself, he gave meaning to his otherwise worthless existence." Alex had just quoted her own written report. If Raymond's reaction was any indication, she was sure to get an A.

Impressed, Raymond paused thoughtfully. "Pretty powerful stuff. No wonder people keep reading these old books."

Alex nodded. "It sure made me stop and think."

"So that's why you've been sleeping on the job." Louis appeared behind Alex's chair and perched on the end of the table. "Too much serious thinking does wear a person out. I try to avoid it as much as possible."

"Hi, Louis," Alex said.

"Glad you're feeling better," Raymond said,

clasping Louis's arm in a mutual shake. "I didn't see you in math this morning, though."

"Just got here. Had to show up so I wouldn't miss the big dance tonight. Better eat, Alex," Louis said, hungrily eyeing her lunch tray. "You've only got a few minutes left before the bell."

"Help yourself." Alex pushed the tray toward Louis. She had snacked constantly during the night to keep awake. "I'm not hungry."

"Thanks." Dropping onto the bench opposite Raymond, Louis unwrapped Alex's sandwich. "You two going to the dance solo or do you have dates?"

"Strictly solo." Raymond raised his hands, then cast a questioning glance at Alex.

"Me, too." Alex decided not to mention getting a ride with Scott. Technically, she *didn't* have a date.

"Excellent." Raymond nodded in approval.

"Yeah. Solo is the only way to go." Louis chewed without looking up, trying to appear casual about the conversation. "A date would just cramp my style."

Alex smiled. Louis probably still felt like the new kid in town, and he didn't want to do anything that would be considered uncool. Like showing up at the dance alone.

"Later, guys. I don't want to be late for class." Yawning again, Alex rose to leave.

"I'm right behind you," Raymond said.

Delayed because she had to stop by her locker to get her books, Alex sank into her seat in English class just as the bell rang. Mrs. Ward gave the class most of the period to read over their book reports. Alex made a few minor corrections on her paper, then struggled to keep from dozing off.

"Here, Alex. This will keep you from falling asleep."

Jerking awake for about the eighth time, Alex looked behind her. Michael Murphy pressed a cartoon calendar into her hand, then quickly turned back to his work.

Alex read the first cartoon, stifled a laugh, then glanced back. With reddish-brown hair, blue eyes, and a spattering of freckles, Michael was really quite good-looking. She wondered why she had never noticed before.

"Attention class." Mrs. Ward clapped her hands as the classroom door opened. "We have some visitors today with some very exciting news."

Alex gasped as Vince and Dave walked in. Raymond didn't flinch, but Nicole sat back in surprise. Sitting two seats in front of her, Robyn stiffened. She looked back, and Alex shrugged. What seemed like another bizarre and mysterious coincidence to Robyn made perfect sense to Alex. Danielle Atron had some new plan to catch her.

Only this time the situation is much worse than usual, Alex thought as Vince and Dave positioned themselves in front of the blackboard. *I'm trapped!*

"Danielle Atron has decided to publish the three best reports in the Paradise Valley Chemical newsletter as book reviews," Mrs. Ward explained.

There was a smattering of applause, which Vince accepted with a nod, but he discreetly avoided meeting anyone's gaze. Dave just looked around as though he had never seen a classroom before.

Alex stared at her desk, wondering. Showcasing book reports in the plant paper was the kind of thing Danielle Atron did all the time to boost the company's benevolent image in the community. It seemed harmless enough. There certainly wasn't anything in her report that proved or even hinted that she was the GC 161 kid. Still, it wouldn't hurt to be cautious.

The warning bell rang, and Mrs. Ward instructed everyone to leave their reports on her desk as they filed out. Alex watched the kids ahead of her, noting their reactions so her behavior wouldn't stand out and draw Vince's suspicious scrutiny. Most just dropped off their reports and began talking with friends as they left. A few nodded or smiled at Vince.

Robyn was in line two kids ahead of Alex. Her report slipped from her hand and fell on the floor just as she reached the desk. Stooping, Robyn quickly scooped it up. Alex noticed that Robyn's hand was shaking as she dropped it on top of the pile. Then she hurried out of the room without smiling or speaking to anyone.

Alex certainly didn't blame Robyn for being nervous. Vince had that effect on people, and she had run into him once too often under very odd circumstances during the past twenty-four hours. Vince and Dave both flicked glances at Robyn as she fled. Alex forced herself to stay calm and decided to ignore them. She absolutely could not do anything that made her look guilty.

As Alex placed her report on the desk, she realized she still had Michael's calendar. *Perfect.* She paused, then gave it back after Michael deposited his report.

"Thanks, Michael," Alex said as he took the calendar. "I was up most of the night finishing this project. Guess I'm a lot more tired than I thought." She kept her gaze on Michael and smiled as they moved toward the door together.

"You're, uh, not too tired, I hope." Michael faltered. "I mean, uh—" Breathing deeply, he finally looked at her and spoke hurriedly. "Are you going to the dance?"

"Yes, I am." Alex paused in the hall outside

the classroom. She had to disappear before Vince and Dave came out, but she didn't want to brush Michael off too abruptly. "I'll see you there."

As she started to turn away, Michael nervously stepped into her path and said, "Great. Uh, maybe we could, uh—dance or something."

"I'd love to."

"Yeah?" Standing taller, Michael met her gaze with large, twinkling blue eyes and grinned.

Alex blinked. Michael Murphy had transformed from a timid dweeb into a confident hunk right before her eyes. *Just because I agreed to dance with him?* Apparently, Robyn was right and Michael really did like her, but she had never dreamed that she could have such a major effect on a boy!

"Guess I'd better go," Michael said. "I don't want to be late for my next class." Michael strode down the hall a few steps, then turned back. "Not that I'd mind talking to you awhile longer."

Alex smiled and said, "You'd better go before the bell rings."

"Yeah, I guess you're right," Michael said,

making a sad face. Waving, he vanished into the crowd.

As Alex turned to leave, Vince stepped from the classroom, saying, "Thank you, Mrs. Ward. Just call my office when you get through grading those reports."

Alex flattened herself against the lockers.

"It won't be long now, Dave." Vince did not even glance at her as he walked past.

Curious, Alex thought, *and very disturbing*. Either Vince was being extra careful to make it look like he didn't notice her or something else was going on. Given everything that had happened since yesterday, Alex was pretty sure they were laying a trap for her. She had to know what they were planning to protect herself. Getting detention for being late to math was a small price to pay for survival.

Caught in the student jam, Vince and Dave had not gotten far. Alex joined the rush behind them. When the bell rang, the hall emptied instantly as kids ducked into their seventh period classes. Alex kept walking as Vince and Dave pushed through the outside doors. She was one row of lockers away from the exit when Mrs. Clark's classroom door opened right behind her. The history teacher paused in the doorway, then stepped back inside the room as though she had forgotten something. It was Mrs. Clark's free period and she was probably going to the lounge or the office.

Alex couldn't let herself be seen. She was positive Mrs. Clark would stop her to ask why she wasn't in class, and Alex had no time for that. She had to catch Vince and Dave before they left the parking lot.

There was only one thing to do. Alex morphed, pushing the limits of her energies to complete the change in record time. A warm tingling rushed from her toes and fingers and spread through her body as solid cells became liquid.

Just as Alex puddled on the floor, Mrs. Clark stepped into the hall.

Alex immediately oozed through the vent holes of the nearest locker. Squeezing through such a narrow opening at high speed created a slight slurping noise.

"What was that?" Mrs. Clark walked to the locker and jiggled the handle. "Who's in there?"

Alex didn't have time to wait her out. The lockers were vented on the sides, too, and she took off through the small slits like a jet-propelled ribbon of slime. She oozed over back-packs, old lunches, sneakers, and soda cans till she reached the end of the line. Then Alex eased a small bit of herself through the vent and saw Mrs. Clark shrug and walk around the corner. Surging through the slits into the empty hall, Alex streaked under the doors and into the juni-per bushes on the side of the building.

Vince and Dave had just stepped off the lawn onto pavement.

Elongating herself, Alex sped across the school grounds like a silvery snake. The plant humvee was parked on the edge of the lot facing a land-scaped divider. As Vince unlocked the door, Alex slid into hiding in front of the vehicle.

"Are we still going to the dance tonight?" Dave asked as he walked in front of the humvee to reach the passenger side.

Alex gurgled a gasp as Dave stepped over her,

but the sound was lost in Vince's impatient response. Alex wasn't sure which upset her more . . . almost being stepped on by Dave or finding out that Vince was going to be at the dance.

"Yes, why wouldn't we?"

"Well . . ." Dave shrugged. "I thought you might want to back out because we know the kid's name—"

"Next time don't think, okay?" Vince yanked open the humvee door. "We still don't have solid evidence, but we'll get it. We'll be watching her like hawks tonight, and she'll buckle under the pressure. She *knows* we suspect she's the one you doused with GC 161, and she's getting nervous. Nervous kids make mistakes."

Don't count on it, Vince, Alex thought resolutely.

"What about the book report? That's solid evidence," Dave said.

Alex rippled in confusion. What did her book report have to do with anything?

"So we matched the page we found to the kid's book report and now we know her name," Vince said. "And we also know that she wasn't checked out with the handprint ID unit. But none of that *proves* anything. How come you're so anxious to close this case all of a sudden?" Vince asked suspiciously.

"I really want to go back to driving a truck, Vince, and I can't do that until you nail the kid."

"Don't worry. She's been lucky so far, but—" Vince looked back toward the school. "Tonight Russo's days of making a fool out of me are over."

Stunned, Alex went rigid.

Vince thought *Robyn* was the GC 161 kid!

CHAPTER 8

Slithering under a leafless bush, Alex huddled in a devastated daze as Vince started the humvee's engine, then backed out of the parking space. When they were gone, she materialized and headed back toward the school. She didn't know how she was going to explain being absent from class, but getting detention was the least of her worries at the moment.

Vince and Dave were tracking Robyn, and Alex felt sure she was responsible. If she hadn't dumped Robyn's backpack, Robyn wouldn't have been in the middle of the street picking up the papers of her report when the truck came barreling toward her.

Their focus on Robyn made perfect sense, too. Dave had almost hit Robyn in exactly the same way and at exactly the same spot as he'd hit Alex when the GC 161 accident occurred. Plus, Robyn had been wearing Alex's hat! Besides, Alex realized, Dave didn't know what color her hair was because it had been covered with gold gunk.

Vince and Dave must have found Robyn's missing book report page in the street, Alex figured, and that's why they wanted to see the reports in class—to match the page and identify the author. And on top of all that, Robyn was so freaked out about the two men popping up everywhere, she was acting really nervous around them—which made her *look* guilty.

Head hanging, Alex went back into the building and trudged toward math class. Her mind raced as she tried to figure out just how bad the situation was.

Vince and Dave were going to be at the dance, but Vince had been very definite about getting positive proof before he took action. This made Alex feel a little better. Robyn wasn't the right kid, so maybe there wasn't anything to worry about. There *wasn't* any positive proof for Vince to get!

"Ms. Mack!" Mr. Krantz, Alex's seventh-grade science teacher, planted himself in front of her. "Pass, please."

"I don't have one," Alex mumbled.

"Why not?"

"Uh, you're not going to believe this, Mr. Krantz, but—"

"Try me."

Alex plunged ahead with the first thing that came to mind. If he didn't believe her, she'd be no worse off than she was now.

"I got locked in the girl's restroom. The door jammed or something. It took me all this time to get out."

Mr. Krantz stared at her over the rim of his glasses. "A likely story. But, you don't make a habit of being tardy, as I recall."

"No, sir. I'm supposed to be in math. That's

where I'm going. Right down there." Alex pointed.

"All right. Come on."

Alex lapsed back into pensive thought as she followed Mr. Krantz. Because the science teacher opened the door for her, the math teacher allowed her to take her seat without an explanation. Alex could not, however, concentrate on math.

On further reflection, Alex realized that she didn't know what *kind* of evidence Vince was talking about. How was he going to gather his evidence? Did he have a plan?

To complicate things, Robyn had a way of overreacting to events large or small. She *would* be the primary target of Vince's surveillance at the dance. Alex had no doubt that when Robyn realized she was being watched, she would get even more nervous, which might make Vince think she was hiding something. And *that* might be all the *proof* Vince needed to drag Robyn into the plant laboratory to be tested.

A shudder coursed through Alex. A true friend, Robyn had only wanted to make her life easier by helping her overcome her faults. But she had returned the favor with anger, and made her pack fall, and now Robyn's life might become a nightmare.

Alex could not let anything bad happen to her friend—no matter what.

Slumping in her chair, she buried her face in her math book. The printed text blurred as her course became clear. She would have to make sure Robyn stayed calm at the dance. Maybe then Vince would realize he was chasing the wrong kid.

Alex could only hope that would be enough.

CHAPTER 9

The gym was in chaos when Alex arrived to help decorate. Exhausted and emotionally drained, she sat on the bottom of the bleachers to wait until things settled down.

The boys who had gym eighth period were frantically removing mats and gymnastic equipment from the floor. A dozen other kids waited on the sidelines with bags of crepe paper and balloons. Robyn's friend, Jerry, sat in a corner cutting out paper hearts at a furious rate. Nicole came in through a side door and held it open for Raymond and Louis. As they carried in a helium canister, Jerry waved at Raymond. Ray let go of the canister to wave back, and the canister almost dropped to the ground.

"Watch it, Raymond!" Louis buckled slightly.

Raymond caught the tilting canister before it crashed, then shrugged sheepishly. Nicole shook her head.

Deciding to make herself useful cutting hearts, Alex hurried along the perimeter of the basketball court. She saw Mr. Krantz, who was the faculty adviser for the dance, and Robyn on the other side of the gym. Robyn looked totally stressed out.

Dodging two boys carrying a rolled up mat, Alex darted across the floor toward Robyn.

"I'm sorry, Mr. Krantz," Robyn said. "I just didn't expect this delay. The dance starts in *four* hours!"

"Everything will be fine, Robyn," Mr. Krantz said patiently. "You're doing a great job. I'll see what I can do to speed things up, okay?"

Nodding, Robyn folded her arms across her stomach as Mr. Krantz called on several boys to lend a hand stacking the equipment against the walls.

"Are you feeling all right?" Alex asked. Robyn looked pale and she was trembling.

"No, I'm not." Shaking her head, Robyn sighed dismally. "It's going to take *hours* to hang all these decorations. If I'm lucky, I'll have maybe fifteen minutes to get dressed after I get home. I hate being rushed."

"We'll get it done in plenty of time, Robyn. Relax." Alex smiled reassuringly, hiding her own tension.

"I think I'm going to be sick," Robyn said. She clutched her stomach and doubled over, then looked up with a stricken expression. "What if I've got the flu?"

"You don't have the flu." Nicole planted herself in front of Robyn. "It's just nerves."

"I don't know, Nicole...." Straightening, Robyn exhaled, then breathed in deeply. "Maybe I caught that germ going around."

"Robyn, you're the chairperson of the decoration committee." Nicole said, folding her arms in front of her chest. "If we don't finish or everyone hates how the gym looks, it will be all your fault. Of course it's nerves!"

"That's supposed to make me feel better?" Robyn rolled her eyes at Alex.

"You're not sick," Nicole said flatly. "You're just worried sick. So quit worrying."

"And if we'd all stop talking and get busy, time won't be a problem either," Alex added enthusiastically. "There's lots of stuff we can get done while we're waiting for those guys to stash the gymnastics equipment."

"You two are the best friends anyone ever had," Robyn said. "What would I do without you?"

Well, for one thing, Alex thought glumly, *you wouldn't have to worry about becoming Danielle Atron's GC 161 test subject of the week.*

"If it's okay with you," Alex said, "I'll cut hearts. Jerry and Elizabeth look like they could use some help."

"Go to it." Robyn glanced at several cardboard boxes piled by the door. "As soon as I find the tape in all this mess, you can start sticking the hearts on the wall, too."

"Here, Alex." Nicole handed a silver choker to Alex.

"Thanks!"

"Did you buy that tape made out of recycled products?" Nicole asked Robyn as Alex put the choker in her pocket.

"Uh, no. I couldn't," Robyn said with a shrug. "I had to get this cheap generic stuff at the discount store."

"How come?" Nicole pressed.

"Because I was running out of time and I had to stay within the decoration committee's budget," Robyn explained. "Renting the wind machine for the grand finale cost a bundle!"

"Oh. Well, I guess it's okay...." Nicole frowned uncertainly. "Just this once."

"Maybe we can recycle the hearts," Alex said, trying to smooth things out. Then she hurried over to join the group cutting hearts, amused by Nicole's dilemma. The wind machine had been Nicole's idea, so she couldn't blame Robyn for the tape.

At least decorating the gym had taken Robyn's mind off Vince and Dave, Alex thought gratefully.

She'd decided not to mention that they would be at the dance. Robyn couldn't stand the additional pressure right now. Besides, she might be so concerned about the decorations and having such a great time with Jerry that she wouldn't even notice that Vince and Dave were masquerading as roadies for the band. Then she wouldn't freak out and there wouldn't be a problem.

Raymond had joined the paper heart brigade, too. As Alex seated herself on the floor beside him, she pushed the more unpleasant possibilities out of her mind. She would deal with those when she had to—*if* she had to.

"Scissors," Raymond said, slapping the grip end into Alex's hand as though she were a surgeon waiting to operate. "Paper."

Jerry made a grand gesture of handing her a piece of red construction paper.

"Cut!" Raymond immediately began to cut with exaggerated care and concentration.

Alex laughed, then lowered her gaze so he wouldn't see the worry in her eyes. Only one thing was certain. She would not let Robyn down again.

* * *

It was almost six by the time Alex got home. Dumping her books on the couch, she rushed into the kitchen and set a grocery bag on the counter. "Hi, Mom."

"Hi, honey." Mrs. Mack looked up from a pile of mail and glanced at the clock. "You're cutting it a little close, aren't you? Annie said your date is picking you up at seven-fifteen."

"It's not a date, Mom. Scott's just giving me a ride." Pulling three boxes of brownie mix out of the bag, Alex scanned the directions and turned on the oven.

"Scott?" Mrs. Mack said. "That nice-looking boy who helped out at the fountain dedication?"

"Yeah." Sighing, Alex read step 2. She had been so focused on protecting Robyn the past few hours, she had hardly thought about Scott.

"What are you doing, honey?" Mrs. Mack asked.

"Making brownies." Alex opened a lower cabinet and dug out two nine-by-thirteen inch baking tins. "I promised Scott I'd bring them. It was an emergency—sort of."

"A brownie emergency?" Mrs. Mack raised an eyebrow.

"Well, yeah. You know how Raymond likes to eat. If there's not enough food at the dance, it might cause a major riot."

"I can imagine."

"Anyway, Scott's the chairperson of the refreshment committee, and Kelly was supposed to bring the brownies, but she got sick, so I'm helping him out." Alex held up a rectangular glass dish. "Can I use this in the oven?"

"Yes." Rising, Mrs. Mack walked over to the counter. "You don't have much time, Alex. Why didn't you come home sooner?"

"I had to help Robyn decorate the gym. I kinda owed her a favor." Alex opened an upper cabinet and pulled out a liquid measuring cup and a large mixing bowl. "Can I mix all three boxes at the same time? Is this bowl big enough?"

Mrs. Mack picked up a box and read the directions. "This looks simple enough. Tell you what—"

"What?" Alex asked absently as she filled the measuring cup with water and set it down. She stared at the one-cup mark, waiting for the water to stop sloshing. "Does it have to be exactly one-third cup for each box?"

"It helps." Mrs. Mack smiled.

Taking the egg carton out of the refrigerator, Alex set it by the bowl and glanced at the red oven light. "How long does it usually take for the oven to finish preheating?"

"Not long." Mrs. Mack opened the brownie mix box. "You kind of like Scott, huh?"

Alex shrugged and took a long wooden spoon out of the utensil drawer. "He's a nice guy."

"Cute, too." Mrs. Mack slipped the spoon out of Alex's hand. "Go on upstairs and start getting ready. I'll put the brownies in the oven."

"You will?" Alex beamed with surprise.

"Sure. Your dad won't be home for another ten minutes or so, and he's taking me out to dinner for Valentine's Day. Besides, I owe Robyn and Scott a favor myself—for helping *me* out when the caterers canceled for the fountain reception."

"Thanks, Mom. You're the greatest." Giving

Mrs. Mack a quick hug, Alex bolted from the kitchen and up the stairs.

Annie wasn't home from the library yet, and Alex welcomed the peace and quiet. She ran a warm bath and set a time limit of fifteen minutes to soak. The warm bubble bath soothed her exhausted body and troubled mind, and she felt herself drifting off. Shaking herself awake, Alex casually altered the molecular structure of her body and liquified. After a year and a half of practice, morphing had become as second nature to her as slipping in and out of clothes was to everyone else. She had never fallen asleep in her liquid form, and taking a bath as a lump of jello always made her feel super clean inside and out. Her relaxed state must have been just what she needed to get her creative juices flowing, because seemingly out of nowhere, an idea came to Alex—a sure way of keeping Robyn out of trouble.

"Alex?" Mrs. Mack knocked, jolting her out of her bubble.

"Just a minute . . ." Alex gurgled and instantly started to solidify.

"Are you all right, Alex? You sound funny."

Mrs. Mack raised her voice to be heard through the closed door. "Alex?"

Materializing under water, Alex surfaced suddenly and wiped water off her face. "I'm fine."

"The brownies are in the oven, and the timer's set. They'll be done in twenty minutes."

"Thanks, Mom."

"Your father and I are leaving now, but Annie should be home soon. Have fun."

Twenty minutes later Alex was dressed and ready except for her hair. It hung down her back in limp, damp strands as she turned off the timer buzzer and opened the oven door.

"Sure smells good in here." Annie walked in, dropped her books on the table, then peered over Alex's shoulder. "Going on a brownie binge?"

"They're for the dance." Alex carefully pulled the hot dishes from the oven and set them on the stove. "The directions said to let them cool before cutting, but Scott's going to be here in half an hour. Is that enough time?"

"Don't know, but the edges get all raggedy and they fall apart if they're too hot. I suppose we could put them in the refrigerator." Annie stepped back. "I'd be more worried about my hair, if I were you. It's still wet!"

"I haven't had a chance to dry it. Nicole was going to do it for me, but she was running late, too. Guess I'll just have to wear it down as usual." It didn't really matter, Alex realized. Crumbling brownies, limp hair, and impressing Scott would not matter at all if Vince and Dave decided Robyn was the GC 161 kid.

"Come on." Annie turned her toward the stairs after she slipped the third dish of brownies into the refrigerator. "I'll take care of the brownies while you go fix your hair. OK?"

Nodding, Alex let Annie push her away. She didn't dare tell Annie that Danielle Atron's security men suspected Robyn or what she planned to do. Annie might try to talk her out of it, and this decision was hard enough without having to defend it. Besides, there wasn't anything Annie could do to help. Even if Annie said that Robyn should be told about the GC 161 accident, knowing that she was under suspicion might cause Robyn to lose it completely.

There was only one thing to do. Alex had created the problem and she had to solve it. She *was* responsible for her own actions, and she was prepared to pay the price for losing her temper and using her powers foolishly. In the end, if the worst happened, she would not have a choice.

Alex had made her decision. If Vince made any threatening moves against Robyn, Alex would just have to turn herself in.

CHAPTER 10

"I think I've met your father a few times, Alex," Scott's dad said. "He's in research and development, isn't he?"

"Yes, he is." Alex didn't know if Scott's father was aware of the secret GC 161 project George Mack was in charge of, but it was best, she decided, not to bring it up.

Scott jumped in to cover the strained silence that followed. "I talked to Tim right before we left the house. He said you guys did a great job decorating the gym."

"He should tell Robyn. She's been a basket

case over those decorations for a week." Alex smiled. "Make that a month.

Scott laughed.

The ride had gone better than Alex had dared hope. Scott had kept a friendly conversation going, and she had even relaxed after the first few minutes. Considering that tonight might be her last night as a "normal" teenager, Alex was in a good mood by the time Scott's father pulled up in front of the gym.

"You kids have a good time," he said.

"We will, and thanks again for the ride." Alex said. She climbed out of the car and turned to find Scott waiting for her.

"You look really fantastic tonight, Alex."

"Thanks, Scott." Startled, Alex didn't know what else to say. She stood frozen in place and just stared at him. She didn't realize she was shivering in the crisp February air until Scott spoke.

"You're cold," he said with a concerned frown. "Come on. Let's get inside."

"It is a little chilly," Alex said, falling into step

beside him. As they headed toward the doors, three ninth-grade girls came running out.

"Hey, Scott! It's about time!"

One of the girls took the brownie tray from Alex and said, "Thanks for making these at the last minute."

"No problem . . ." Alex was pushed back as the girls surrounded Scott and urged him inside.

Just before he disappeared through the doors, Scott looked back. "Catch ya later, Alex."

"Later." Trailing behind, Alex entered the gym by herself. *So much for my grand entrance with Scott.* Pausing in the doorway, she looked over the gym.

Scott had already taken control of the refreshment table at one end of the room. Risers formed a stage at the other end, and four men wearing dark pants and long-sleeved, open-necked shirts were testing their musical equipment. Robyn and Jerry walked along the far wall, inspecting the decorations. A paper heart fell at Robyn's feet and she hastily stuck it back up. Watching, Alex's resolve was strengthened. Although she was still reeling from Scott's attentive interest, Robyn was her first priority.

"Yo, Alex!" Louis suddenly appeared on one side of her and Raymond on the other.

"Lookin' sharp, Alex." Raymond nodded with a wide grin.

"I'll say." Louis fell on one knee in front of her. "Dance with me. Now—before my heart breaks."

"The music hasn't even started yet, Louis," Alex pointed out.

"True." Jumping to his feet, Louis turned toward the refreshment table. "Guess I'll get something to eat."

"There's Elizabeth Hunter over by the stage," Alex said. "I think she likes you, Ray."

"Really?" Raymond's eyebrows shot up. Then he tried to look casual as he said, "What's not to like?" He glanced toward the stage, seeing Elizabeth wave. "Watch me in action," he said as he smoothed his hair.

As Raymond casually walked to the far end of the gym, Alex went to join Robyn and Jerry in a corner with Nicole. A large, rented wind fan sat on the floor and the electrical cord dangled from Nicole's hand. Both girls looked distressed.

"What's the problem?" Alex asked.

"What isn't the problem?" Robyn huffed in exasperation. A paper heart drifted down from above and rested on her shoulder. She slapped it back on the wall, then pounded it with her fist for good measure. "All the hearts are falling down because I bought this cheap tape that doesn't stay stuck!"

"They aren't *all* falling, Robyn," Jerry said. "Just one or two here and there."

"Look at it this way," Nicole said matter-of-factly. "It'll be real easy to undecorate if half the decorations are already on the floor."

Crossing her arms, Robyn rolled her eyes and tapped her foot.

"Plugging in this fan is a bigger problem. No fan, no grand finale for the balloons." Nicole sighed and looked up.

Alex followed her gaze and saw a large net filled with balloons hanging from the ceiling directly above.

Then Alex looked at Robyn, and her spirits

sank. *Robyn is falling apart over hearts and fans, and Vince and Dave aren't even here yet! What will she do when they arrive?*

"Why can't you plug it in?" Alex asked.

"The outlet is behind all that stuff." Nicole gestured toward the huge pile of gymnastics equipment that had been shoved against the wall and covered with a tarp. "It's way too heavy to move. And where would we put it all, if we did move it?"

"Why not just use the one down there?" Jerry pointed to an outlet halfway down the side wall.

"Can't," Nicole said. "The fan has to be in *this* corner or the balloons will just fall *here* instead of being blown all over the gym when we release them at the end of the dance." Nicole sighed again. "It's my fault for hanging them there without checking the outlet first."

"I'll take care of it," Alex said quickly. She felt it was the least she could do to help Robyn. "You all take a break. I owe you one for letting me leave before everything was done this afternoon anyway."

"It's all yours." Nicole handed her the cord. "Come on, Robyn. I'm thirsty."

"Me, too." Jerry took Robyn by the arm.

"I'll never volunteer to be chairperson of anything again," Robyn said as Jerry led her away. "It's just asking for trouble."

Alone again, Alex checked to make sure no one was watching. Squatting behind the gym equipment to hide her actions, she telekinetically maneuvered the cord into the narrow space and pushed the plug into the outlet. Maybe she could convince anyone who asked that she was slim enough to edge behind the stack and that her arm was just long enough to reach.

Alex was just about to stand up when a voice above her asked, "Lose something?"

Alex snapped her head around and inhaled sharply.

Dave smiled down at her.

CHAPTER 11

Dave was wearing a fake mustache, dark pants, and a blue vest over a white shirt, but Alex recognized him instantly.

"Uh—no. Just, uh—" Stumped, Alex looked down at the silver sandals Annie had loaned her because they matched Nicole's choker and the silver ribbon in her hair. "Just tightening the buckle on my shoe."

"Come on!" Vince grabbed Dave by the arm and pulled him away. "The band was ready to start five minutes ago." Dark sunglasses and an old fedora was the extent of Vince's costume. He still wore his usual office get-up.

Again, Alex realized with great relief that Vince had no interest in her, just like when he'd seen her at school. As the two men darted to the equipment set up beside the stage, Alex went to find Robyn. She was talking with Raymond and Louis while she waited for Jerry to get back from the boys' room.

"The fan's plugged in," Alex said.

"It is? How'd you manage that? No—" Robyn held up her hand. "I don't need to know."

Relaxing, Alex scanned the room as the band began to play. Small groups of kids slowly moved onto the floor to dance.

"This should be good," Raymond said. "Steel Wool is the hottest band around."

"That guy doesn't look so cool," Louis said, pointing at Vince.

Alex looked toward the stage as Vince leaned down to untangle some electronic cords. His sunglasses slid down his nose and as he straightened back up, the hat fell off.

"It's that guy!" Robyn said. "Vince, from the

plant. And that's the other one! What are they doing here?"

Worried, Raymond looked at Alex. He didn't know Vince and Dave suspected Robyn and obviously thought they were on the scene looking for Alex instead.

"It's not a big deal," Alex said casually. "Vince and Dave are always around when Danielle Atron sponsors something. She's paying for the band."

Robyn wasn't convinced. "But ever since they almost ran me down yesterday, they seem to show up everywhere I go." Her eyes widened and she lowered her voice to a whisper. "Maybe they're afraid I'll tell Danielle Atron how they almost hit me. Maybe they've decided to shut me up—permanently."

"Because of an accident that *didn't* happen?" Alex said. "I doubt it." Alex thought frantically of a way to calm Robyn down. "They'd be after all of us then. We were witnesses."

"Alex is right," Raymond said. "Danielle is probably just trying to save a few bucks by having them help out."

"Well, I hope so." Robyn shuddered. "It's really creepy running into them all the time."

"What are you guys standing around for?" Jerry returned and took Robyn's hand. "This is a dance!"

While everyone else rushed out onto the dance floor, Alex found a chair near the corner with the fan and sat down. She needed a few minutes alone to recharge. Keeping Robyn calm was a physical drain, and she was already overtired from lack of sleep.

And the situation was not improving. Alex hadn't considered how Robyn would be affected if Vince didn't get conclusive evidence tonight that she either was or wasn't the GC 161 kid. As long as they suspected her, they would be like perpetual, dark shadows always lurking around the corner and showing up in unexpected places. Robyn wouldn't have a moment's peace.

Alex couldn't let that happen, either. Poor Robyn wouldn't know why she was being watched and harassed, and it would drive her completely nuts.

Alex's thoughts were rudely interrupted by a

loud, distorted voice booming through the band's PA system. The lead guitar player stopped singing to glare at Vince, who was frantically moving levers on the electronic equipment.

The keyboard player jumped down from the stage, and Vince stepped aside to let him make adjustments on the board. The bass player and lead guitarist rolled their eyes at each other.

"So what happened with Scott?" Nicole asked as she sat down next to Alex.

"Well, he told me I looked fantastic tonight. Can you believe that, Nicole?"

Nicole gave her a high-five. "Yes, I can," she said. "But then why are you sitting here on the sidelines?"

"Scott's a little busy." Alex glanced toward the refreshment table. There were almost as many kids standing in line for food and drinks as there were on the dance floor. It didn't look like Scott was going to get a break any time soon.

Nicole shrugged. "So dance with someone else."

"I will. Have you seen Michael?"

"Michael Murphy? No, I haven't, but when I do, I'll send him right over. Uh-oh." Nicole quickly stood up. "There's Douglas Potts. I sort of promised to dance with him. See you later."

Leaning back, Alex shook her head.

A red paper heart drifted down into Alex's lap. *An omen?* Holding it, Alex closed her eyes and imagined dancing with Scott. She pictured herself in Scott's arms, moving around the floor in slow motion, eyes only for each other in soft, hazy lighting with a thousand paper hearts swirling gently all around them. She wanted so much for Scott to like her. . . .

She felt a *click* in her head and didn't think anything of it until it was too late to stop the telekinetic surge her intense wishing had triggered.

Suddenly, the crowd was squealing with delight and awe.

Opening her eyes, Alex gasped.

Paper hearts were lifting off the walls and floating through the air in lazy swirls just as she had imagined in her fantasy! It had happened again! A renegade telekinetic burst had turned her thoughts into reality.

Alex took everything in with one sweeping glance.

Almost everyone was laughing and thoroughly enjoying the show as paper hearts drifted in graceful swirls through the air and around the dancers.

Robyn stood in the middle of the dance floor, watching the scene with an expression that shifted between wonder and worry.

The band was between songs, and Vince was staring at Robyn.

There's no way to explain this, Alex thought, her heart and mind racing. *Or is there?*

Rising, Alex concentrated on the large wind fan sitting on the floor twenty feet away and telekinetically turned it on. The powerful stream of forced air kept the falling hearts from settling to the floor. Then Alex immediately hurried over to the fan. Maybe no one would notice that she hadn't been standing there all along.

Bewildered, Robyn hesitated as the crowd moved back toward the edges of the gym and cheered the display with whistles and thunderous applause. The drummer added his two cents worth with a drum roll and smashing cymbals.

Alex held her breath as Vince brushed paper hearts off the soundboard, then turned to stare at Robyn again.

Jerry noticed Alex standing by the fan. He chuckled and nudged Robyn. A slow smile spread across Robyn's face, and she nodded as her gaze locked with Alex's. Alex was pretty sure Robyn thought she had deliberately turned on the fan when the hearts started falling off the walls because of the faulty tape. Alex gave her a thumbs up and shrugged. It was great to see Robyn smiling instead of fretting.

Nicole and Douglas skirted the dancers, making their way to the corner as Raymond and Louis crossed in front of the stage. They all converged on Alex as she flipped the fan switch off.

"Pretty slick, Alex," Nicole said. "You turned a potential disaster into a totally cool scene for Robyn."

"That's the truth." Raymond looked at her askance, obviously wondering if there was more to the story than Alex was telling.

"Really great special effects," Douglas said.

Nodding, Alex kept a wary eye on Robyn. Urged on by the crowd, Robyn turned in a slow circle and bowed. Then, as she faced the band and saw Vince staring at her, Robyn grabbed Jerry and bolted from the center of the room. Mr. Krantz intercepted them to shake Robyn's hand, but she quickly broke away, leaving the baffled chaperon scratching his bald head.

"Did my hair suddenly develop a major case of frizzies?" Robyn asked as she and Jerry joined the group. "Did I bust a seam or what?"

"No, you look great. Why?" Jerry asked.

"Because that Vince guy keeps staring at me like I'm going to steal his stupid equipment or something!" Robyn's high-pitched voice carried as she pointed.

Mr. Krantz, nearby, turned to angrily glare at Vince.

Noticing the teacher, Vince quickly averted his gaze and moved around the soundboard. As the band launched into another song, Vince tripped over a mike cord, unplugging it just as the guitar player started to sing. Only the instruments sounded through the loudspeakers.

"They should have left that roadie home!" Louis said as the singer tapped the microphone to confirm that it was dead.

"Definitely jinxed," Nicole said.

Dave picked up the disconnected cord, then leaned over and inserted the jack back into the soundboard. Shrill, earsplitting feedback and crackling static blared from the speakers.

A stunned paralysis settled over Alex as events raced out of control around her. She watched helplessly as her doom was sealed in the space of a few, action-packed seconds.

Startled by the unexpected, electronic shrieks, the drummer tossed his drumsticks in the air. Then he fell forward off his stool, knocking over the cymbals.

The clang of crashing metal and high, whistling feedback was too much for Robyn. Clamping her hands over her ears, she pushed into the crowd. "Come on, Jerry. I need some fresh air and a few minutes of peace and quiet!"

The singer threw up his hands, shook his

head, then jumped off the stage to fix the problem.

Ignoring the angry keyboard man, Vince frowned and started walking across the crowded dance floor.

Raymond quickly drew Alex aside. "Vince is headed this way, Alex! You've got to get out of here!"

"He's not after me, Ray!" Alex whispered. "Vince thinks Robyn is the GC 161 accident kid!"

Raymond's eyes widened in shock. "Robyn? How come?"

"I'll explain later . . . if I can." After a quick scan of the gym, Alex was certain she wouldn't get a chance to explain anything to anyone.

Robyn and Jerry were halfway down the side wall, almost to the exit. Nicole and Douglas were weaving through the crowd a short distance behind. And Vince was approaching from another angle.

"Come on, Ray. I've got to do something," Alex said.

"Why? Robyn doesn't have any GC 161 in her system. Vince can't do anything to harm her."

"That's not true, Ray," Alex said with serious calm. "If Vince decides to test her, that would prove she's not the kid. But would you want to go through who-knows-what kind of awful procedures in Danielle Atron's lab?"

Raymond held up his palms. "No, thank you."

"Right. And even if Vince doesn't go that far, as long as he suspects her, he'll never leave her alone. Robyn wouldn't be in this mess if it wasn't for me, and I'm not going to let her take any more of the heat."

"But what can you do about it?"

Edging past him, Alex met Raymond's worried gaze with a look of grim determination. "If I have to, I'll turn myself in."

CHAPTER 12

Alex moved along the wall toward the group closing in on Robyn. Vince was getting closer and closer by the second.

"What's going on?" Louis asked as he fell into line behind Alex and Raymond.

"Hopefully, nothing," Raymond said with a heavy sigh.

As Alex pressed forward, she felt her resolve to turn herself in slipping away. The thought of forfeiting her relatively normal, carefree life to become an experimental pawn in Danielle Atron's quest for wealth and power made her blood run cold. Once she had identified herself, there would be no turning back. She'd become a lab rat in Danielle Atron's cage. Everything she cherished would be gone—forever.

Then Alex thought about Charles Darnay in *A Tale of Two Cities.* He had left his family and the safety of England to help an old friend, even though going back to France put him in dire danger. Then Sidney Carton had sacrificed himself to save Charles. And *they* weren't even responsible for the cruel fates each of them faced.

Alex paused to collect herself. " 'It is a far, far better thing that I do than I have ever done,' " she said softly, quoting the last line of the book.

"James T. Kirk," Louis said brightly. "*Star Trek,* right?"

Alex rolled her eyes toward him. "Sidney Carton. *A Tale of Two Cities.*" Shaking her head at the two boys, she took a deep breath and started forward again.

"Not so fast, Alex," Raymond hissed in her ear.

"It's not like I have a choice, Ray."

"Just take it easy until we know for sure what's happening," Raymond said patiently.

"I am totally confused," Louis muttered.

"That is not a significant problem at the moment," Raymond said. "Uh-oh."

Just ahead, Alex saw Vince jump in front of Robyn. Blocking the door, the head of plant security narrowed his steely blue eyes, and Robyn froze.

"We need to talk, young lady—in private," Vince said firmly.

Alex pushed forward, then hesitated as Jerry protectively placed himself between Robyn and Vince. Nicole and Douglas flanked her on both sides, and all three glared at Vince.

"What's your problem, mister?" Jerry demanded indignantly.

"Why don't you pick on someone your own size?" Nicole said, with her hands on her hips and her chin jutted out.

"She doesn't have to talk to you in private or anywhere else," Douglas stated emphatically. "She has the right to be *secure in her person*. Article Four; the Constitution of the United States."

"Yeah!" Louis added with a scowl, even though he didn't have a clue what all the fuss was about.

Vince flinched, then frowned uncertainly, and Alex realized that he didn't dare create a scene. He couldn't explain *why* he wanted to talk to Robyn, either. No one was supposed to know about the experimental chemical GC 161 except Vince, Dave, Danielle Atron, and her superiors, and it had to stay that way. However, that, too, would only help Robyn out of the immediate situation. It wouldn't keep Vince from following and watching her later.

Alex shriveled inside as each potential escape avenue was closed. She just had to accept the fact that there was only one way to save Robyn from a life of constant harassment. Gritting her teeth, Alex eased between Robyn and Nicole.

"Alex, don't . . ." Raymond pleaded.

"Excuse me, but—" Alex was abruptly cut off as Mr. Krantz stormed into the middle of the group. Dave and the singer paused off to the side.

"*What* is going on here?" Furious, Mr. Krantz aimed the question directly at Vince.

A brittle tension hovered between the two men as they eyed each other. Alex tensed. Both of them were used to being in charge, giving orders instead of taking them. Although Alex thought it would be extremely cool if Vince backed down from the short, balding teacher, she would *still* have to confess in the end. She just wanted to get it over with!

"Nothing's going on," Vince replied.

"Then why are *you*, a grown man, harassing one of my students?" Mr. Krantz stepped closer and poked Vince repeatedly in the shoulder. Alex had never seen him so mad.

"That's what I'd like to know," Robyn mumbled as everyone edged back to give Mr. Krantz room just in case Vince decided to take a swing at him.

Alex stepped closer to her friend and whispered in her ear, "You don't have anything to worry about, Robyn. Just take my word for it, okay?"

"Pardon me." Vince said, smiling at Robyn.

"Do you remember where you were at three-thirty in the afternoon the first day of school last year?"

"Huh?" Robyn blinked.

Vince's question was asked so casually and seemed so irrelevant to the circumstances, that everyone but Dave, Raymond, and Alex just looked at Vince with perplexed expressions.

Alex's throat constricted as she watched Robyn. She couldn't possibly remember what she was doing then, could she?

"Who cares!" Surrounded by friends and defended by Mr. Krantz, Robyn's whole attitude suddenly changed. She leaned toward Vince with fire in her eyes. "I was at the doctor's getting my allergy shot, if you *must* know. And I'm not going to say anything about what *almost* happened yesterday because I don't want any trouble with your boss, either! So leave me alone, okay?"

Surprised and relieved, Alex exhaled and slumped against Raymond. Robyn had an alibi and her doctor's records would confirm it. Vince now knew—positively—that Robyn could not possibly be the kid he was looking for.

"Okay. Thank you."

Dave turned to Vince and shrugged. "Sorry, Vince."

As Vince lunged toward Dave, Mr. Krantz grabbed his shirttail. "Out! Nobody messes with my students and gets away with it!" Mr. Krantz pointed toward the door.

Hoots and whistles followed Vince as he slunk through the exit and disappeared into the night. Then a cheer rang out for Mr. Krantz, who nodded modestly and urged everyone to forget the disturbance and enjoy themselves.

"That was *too* close, Alex," Raymond whispered.

Alex had to agree. All too soon, Vince and Danielle Atron would be plotting another scheme to catch her, but for now—she was safe. More importantly, so was Robyn.

A deejay turned on some CDs while the band was adjusting all the equipment Vince had messed up.

Raymond was instantly in motion. "Later, Alex."

"Hey, Raymond! Wait up. What exactly just happened here?" Louis darted after him.

Sighing, Alex stepped back as Dave and the singer walked by. "I understand you play the drums, Dave," the singer said. "My drummer hurt his wrist when he fell off the stool. You can sit in if you want to—just don't destroy the equipment."

"I won't. Promise." Rubbing his hands together, Dave whooped, then danced toward the stage.

"We're going to get something to munch on, Alex," Robyn said.

"I'm glad you're feeling better," Alex said honestly.

Robyn waved her concern aside. "It could only happen to me. I knew they were afraid I'd say something about the accident, but I think they got the message."

"You told him off but good," Jerry said proudly.

"Why don't you come with us, Alex?" Robyn asked.

Alex glanced toward the refreshment table. Scott and his three helpers were still busy keeping the bowls and platters filled and the hungry crowd under control. Catching her eye, Scott smiled and waved, then shrugged helplessly. Alex waved back. He was stuck for the moment, but it was still early. The dance wasn't even half over yet. Maybe he would ask her to dance, but she'd just have to wait to find out.

"Maybe later, Robyn. But thanks," Alex said.

"There's Michael, Alex." Nicole stood on tiptoe and gestured toward the far side of the gym. "Where's he been anyway?"

"In the boys' room," Jerry said casually.

"All night?" Alex asked incredulously.

Nicole winked at her. "Some people vegetate on the sidelines waiting for Mr. Right, and some people hang out in restrooms because they're shy. Makes perfect sense to me."

"Actually, it doesn't make any sense at all, does it?" Alex grinned sheepishly, then waved and headed across the floor. She had learned a lot from this latest encounter with Vince and Dave.

Never again, under any circumstances, would she use her powers in anger—not even by accident. Now that she knew intense emotions could subconsciously trigger a telekinetic command when she imagined things, she could control it. The *click* she felt in her head was like a red alert, a warning she would recognize in time to disengage the telekinetic surge before it escaped her mind. She did not have to worry about her fantasies becoming unwanted realities again.

Spotting Michael standing alone by the wall, Alex smiled and walked toward him. She had come so close to losing what was most important, that now she realized something else that should have been obvious. Life was much too short to waste even a minute sitting around wishing and waiting for something—or someone—that might never happen.

"Hi, Michael. Wanna dance?"

About the Author

Diana G. Gallagher lives in Kansas with her husband, Marty Burke, two dogs, three cats, and a cranky parrot. When she's not writing, she likes to read and take long walks with the dogs.

A Hugo Award–winning illustrator, she is best known for her series *Woof: The House Dragon.* Her songs about humanity's future are sung throughout the world and have been recorded in cassette form: "Cosmic Concepts More Complete," "Star*Song," and "Fire Dream." Diana and Marty, an Irish folksinger, perform traditional and original music at science-fiction conventions as a duo.

Her first adult novel, *The Alien Dark,* appeared in 1990. She is also the author of a *Star Trek: Deep Space Nine*® novel for young readers, *Arcade,* and four other books in *The Secret World of Alex Mack* series, all available from Minstrel Books.

She is currently working on another *Star Trek* novel and a new *Alex Mack* story.